James M. Stuart, Club Gobden

The History of Free Trade in Tuscany

With remarks on its progress in the rest of Italy

James M. Stuart, Club Gobden

The History of Free Trade in Tuscany
With remarks on its progress in the rest of Italy

ISBN/EAN: 9783337234867

Printed in Europe, USA, Canada, Australia, Japan

Cover: Foto ©Andreas Hilbeck / pixelio.de

More available books at **www.hansebooks.com**

LONDON :

CASSELL PETTER & GALPIN, BELLE SAUVAGE WORKS,

LUDGATE HILL, E.C.

FREE TRADE IN TUSCANY.

THE HISTORY

OF

FREE TRADE IN TUSCANY.

WITH

Remarks on its Progress in the rest of Italy.

BY

JAMES MONTGOMERY STUART.

CASSELL PETTER & GALPIN:
LONDON, PARIS & NEW YORK.

1876.

PREFACE.

THE Committee of the COBDEN CLUB publishes this interesting "History of Free Trade in Tuscany" because it proves clearly how great is the benefit arising from the *practical* application of Free Trade principles. But the Committee, while adhering entirely to them as enunciated by Sallustio Bandini, Adam Smith, Cavour, and Richard Cobden, does not feel itself called upon to decide who among present Italian Statesmen have remained faithful to those principles, and who may have, in a greater or less degree, infringed them.

J. W. PROBYN.

London, April, 1876.

THE HISTORY OF FREE TRADE
IN TUSCANY.

BY JAMES MONTGOMERY STUART.

THE historian who would narrate the progress of political economy, and fix the attention of his readers on its most luminous points, will soon discover that the States most remarkable for their historical importance and territorial extension are not those which offer the most productive field for his labours. He will find that there is here presented another example of what elsewhere meets his eye—that the course of civilisation has been most powerfully helped on by peoples dwelling within a narrow zone of land: now Palestine; again, Attica; many centuries later, Provence;—by the free efforts of small communities like Geneva or Holland; by the learning, the taste, the varied forms of genius that were concentrated at the commencement of the present century in the little duchy of Weimar. But of all the States thus territorially small, but intellectually and morally great, Tuscany, next to Athens, is the greatest. The "All-Etruscan Three" suffice of themselves to usher in the greatest names of mediæval and modern letters. So conspicuous were the Florentines for their genius in the highest State affairs and the most complicated international relations, that the fact has often been illustrated by the anecdote of Pope Boniface VIII., who, one day, after a State reception, in which twelve separate countries were represented by twelve envoys, all Florentines, exclaimed, " Really, these Florentines form a fifth element in creation ! " Nor were the habits of profound speculation and many-sided action which mark the stirring time of the republic lost under the absolute princes of the grand duchy. Rulers who could rank Galileo amongst their personal friends, and to whom the earliest ethical writings of Bacon, in their Italian form, were dedicated, showed that they came of the old stock. Unhappily, the princes of the house of Medici, though individually men of much ability, allowed their entire system of policy to be coloured by their belief that their absolute rule could only be secured through a complete paralysis of all the energies of their subjects ; through the working of a system of feudalism and court intrigue intended to crush out all the old republican traditions; and through the concentration in their own hands of that commercial enterprise which had once given wealth and power to an entire people. Still, much of the old spirit remained unbroken ; and when, after the death of John Gaston, the last prince of the house of Medici, the dominions of that house passed to rulers of German origin, this intellectual primacy only assumed another form, and in the writings of Sallustio Bandini and his school, and the legislative measures that were their direct consequence, the little State of Tuscany led the way in that grand campaign of economical reform, marked by so many alternations of victory and defeat, of which the longest-lived man of the present generation will assuredly not witness the final issue.

The history of the Grand Duchy of Tuscany during a period of more than a hundred and twenty years is emphatically and pre-eminently the history of Free Trade. It is the history of its announcement by private individuals of truly pure and patriotic character ; of its acceptance, not without contending against many difficulties, by the government; of the legislation in which its maxims were fully embodied ; of the beneficent results which it produced ; of its necessary alliance with peace and non-intervention ; of the extraneous influences by which its course was repeatedly arrested ; of the political and domestic re-actions that from time to time sought to stifle it ; and, finally, of its influence on the general, commercial, and political history of the Italian peninsula. Should the treatment of this subject prove dry and unattractive, the fault will be that of the writer—not, assuredly, of the subject itself—for it is not wanting in episodes of its own quite as interesting as those by which the annals of great wars and far-reaching policy are interspersed, and it deals, though in humble proportions, with questions that have in our own day stirred to its very depths the national heart of England, and which lie at the foundation of the material and moral progress of every country in the world.

The central figure in this history is that of the second sovereign of the House of Hapsburgh-Lorraine, the Grand Duke Peter Leopold. And if economists may be allowed equally with lawyers or soldiers to indulge in their own hero-worship, the figure of Peter Leopold may be placed in a niche beside the figures of Justinian and Alexander. Machiavelli has for the uses of practical politics given us a somewhat rough but very convenient division of mankind into three classes—the men who are capable of originating great truths ; the men who, without that capacity, have the power to recognise and the will to apply them ; and the men who have neither original thoughts nor the power of appreciating the thoughts of others. If we cannot assign Peter Leopold to the first of these three classes, it would perhaps be difficult to find another prince in history who more deserves to stand first in the first rank of the second category. Nor will the estimate of his merits be lessened by a calm and impartial review of the task which he undertook, or of the helps, facilities, and preparations by which the work was lightened. Whether among such helps and preparations must be

classed the fact of his being an absolute sovereign, is a
question which may be answered in quite opposite
ways, according as we reproduce to our minds the
resources attached to such a position, or the trials and
temptations by which its holders are beset.

We shall frequently have occasion to observe that
in the growth of Free Trade in Tuscany the traditions
of the ancient manufacturing and commercial glory of
Florence were much more a hindrance than a help.
Florence, the Italian Manchester of the Middle Ages,
owed its wealth and power to its great cloth and silk
manufactures, and to the trade with all parts of the
civilised world consequent on the same. But the cloth
manufacture passed by degrees from the hands of the
Florentines to those of the Flemish and the English ;
and this transference, if we may believe Florentine
writers of eminence, was owing not a little to the short-
sightedness of the Florentines themselves, who, in order
to diminish the cost of the raw material, saved the
expense of transport by establishing branch manufactories in Flanders and England, thereby affording greater
opportunities for the Flemish and English to learn their
processes, and even exposing themselves to the risk
of having their best workmen lured away from their
employment to promote the prosperity of their foreign
rivals. The cloth manufacturers of Florence would not
have found themselves so entirely dependent on foreign
wool if they had held the pursuits of agriculture in a
little more regard. But amongst the most deeply-rooted
prejudices of the manufacturing and mercantile commonwealth was the contempt for rural pursuits, if we
except the slight degree of market and ornamental
gardening required for household wants and holiday
recreation. It has been affirmed on high authority that
these Italian manufacturers and merchants of the Middle
Ages carried on a commerce free at least from the evils
of protectionism ; and the same affirmation has been
made respecting the States of antiquity. The affirmation

must, however, be received with great reserve. It is at variance with the spirit of intense jealousy and bitter rivalry shown towards each other by the mediæval republics, and it is equally at variance with the numberless restrictions by which, in the commercial legislation of ancient Rome, the most important of all trades, that in corn, was surrounded. In a modified form, however, the statement may be accepted, in so far as it reflects not the origin, the immense increase of prohibitions and monopolies in the vast empire of Charles V., and more especially in the Italian States directly or indirectly subject to Spanish rule. But, without discussing how far, after the final overthrow of the Florentine Republic, in 1537, the first princes of the house of Medici contributed to introduce altogether a Protectionist policy, or only to extend and strengthen one which they already found established, it may suffice to state that their relation as rulers to their subjects in a great part of their dominions was that of oppressive masters over a conquered and down-trodden people. Such had already been the relation between the victorious commonwealth of Florence and its vanquished rival, Pisa, which it subjugated and annexed, carrying its hatred of the vanquished foes to the suicidal point of laying a great portion of the territory under water, and, by the complete destruction of the naval resources, destroying a mercantile marine which had furnished the chief appliances and means for its own carrying trade. What the republic had thus done for Pisa the first Grand Duke Cosimo and his immediate successors did for Siena. Ireland, at the worst period of English misgovernment; Poland, when Russia pressed most heavily on the unhappy Poles, may suggest some idea of the spirit in which Siena was ruled by the grand dukes of the house of Medici, after the final destruction, by the Grand Duke Cosimo I., of the Sienese Republic. In one respect the grand dukes strictly maintained in their system of administration the traditions of the Florentine Republic. That republic

entrusted the government of the different communes
which it successively annexed only to Florentine citizens.
All posts of importance, whether administrative, judicial,
or military, were in Florentine hands. The same system
was rigorously carried out by the grand dukes—no-
where with greater rigour than in the territory of Siena.
This province, which, from its physical, commercial,
and social conditions, was destined to play so important
a part in the economic history of Tuscany, had especial
reason to lament its subjection to the Florentine rule.
It was eminently an agricultural district ; the inhabitants
were devoted to agricultural pursuits ; the Sienese
aristocracy, far from sharing the Florentine prejudices
respecting agricultural pursuits, had always prosecuted
them with hearty zeal ; and, as a necessary consequence,
the tone imparted by their new masters to the treatment
of the whole country clashed both with their interests
and habits.

The evils arising from the systematic disregard
shown by the Medicean Princes of the special interests
and wants of the province of Siena were not counter-
balanced by the benefits which they rendered to the
manufacturing and commercial interests of Florence.
The first grand dukes, indeed, professed to be merchants as well as princes ; they carried on business in
several great European cities, but their mercantile character did far more harm than good to the general
mercantile interests of the country. When a despotic
prince goes into the market, whether home or foreign,
as the competitor in trade with his own subjects, he has
certain " Protectionist " influences at his command which
are but too likely at any moment to bring all competition to a standstill. Tuscany, indeed, derived great
benefits from one feature of the Medicean policy—the
creation of the city of Leghorn, and the exceptional
privileges—especially in reference to the free exercise of
religion—accorded to foreign settlers in that port. But
even the usefulness of Leghorn was much hampered

by two facts. Amongst the modes by which the first Grand Duke Cosimo had tried to gain the support of the Court of Rome for the establishment of his dynasty, was the institution of an order of maritime knights, bound by their vows to wage continual war against the Barbary powers. This, of course, provoked retaliation from Constantinople, as well as from Algiers and Tunis. The galleys of the Knights of St. Stephen were, all through the Levant, regarded as the symbols of injury and insult to the Crescent ; the commercial result being that the Levant trade, productive of so much wealth to the Florentine Republic, was hermetically sealed against the grand duchy of Tuscany. But Leghorn suffered in another way. All the favours and privileges of a free port enjoyed by its inhabitants were practically useless for the exchange of Tuscan produce ; for beyond the gates of Leghorn commenced the operation of the complicated and most hurtful system of inland tolls and custom-houses—of all that machinery of wretched legislation by which the exchange of foreign, and, indeed, of native commodities, was rendered difficult in every corner of the grand-ducal territory. Foremost amongst the causes of these difficulties were the conditions of land tenure and the privileges accorded to the Church ; but the old system, as it was found in full force when the Medicean dynasty came to a close, will, perhaps, be better understood if I quote the following passage from the historian who has thus furnished me with its leading features :—

"The twenty-three volumes of the Medicean legislation, collected and annotated by the advocate Lorenzo Cantini, are full of decrees and notifications containing new obstacles, all invented to complicate the machinery of government, already far too much clogged. That machine was composed of elements so numerous, so heterogeneous, and so discordant, that they were constantly clashing with each other, to the very serious injury of public affairs. Some had their origin in republican times, others came from a monarchical and despotic source, so that they had not and could not have the same character, nor any unity in their tendencies. But let us deal with precise facts. The fairest and most widely-extended tracts of land were owned and held in *mortmain* by the regular and secular clergy. There were not a few other castes possessing high rank, with the privilege of creating entails, special rights of primo-geniture, and inalienable pensions., All Tuscany was split up into so many fiefs, some established at a distant period, under the German emperors, but most of them the creation of the Medici. The State of Siena was a fief of Spain. From this state of matters there arose insur-mountable legal barriers to the development of agricul-ture. The privileges secured by the game laws and by the fishery rights were such that the fruits of the soil were often more use to wild animals than to man, and that hydraulic science was prevented from dealing with the streams of water and the stagnant pools in order to render the land healthy and to drain and make available for agriculture excellent and wide-stretching tracts of land. The property of the communes was burdened with the baronial rights of grazing and felling timber. The communes, in their turn, could command the labour of the peasants, and of their animals of draught and burden, for the maintenance of the highways, and for the carriage of materials, for the services known by the name *coman-dati*. Then the vassals were bound to render personal service to their feudal lords. Special taxes in every little district, all of them most burdensome, clogging and hampering the contracts in the disposal of the few rural and urban properties which were left disposable. Cus-tom duties, so high, and at the same time so much divided that the expense of collection swallowed up two-thirds and more of the entire amount, not to speak of the loss of time, of the worry, and the vexation en-dured by those who had to pay them. It was made obligatory to declare the getting-in of all crops, and even the birth of the cattle. It was prohibited to bring either crops or cattle to market until the permission had first been given by the *grascieri*, or officers specially charged with the direction of the food-market. Custom-houses at the frontier, preventing the entrance of the commodities most wanted for internal consumption, and impeding the exit from the grand duchy of the articles and provisions of which the country had a surplus. Intermediate custom-houses between one district and another, arresting at every step the circulation of goods and of provisions in the interior of the country. Then there were whole classes of privileged persons specially exempted from all these odious finance and fiscal annoyances. All the property of the regular and secular clergy, and all the crown lands, were exempted from every species of tax, direct or indirect, ordinary or extraordinary. Monks and nuns of certain privileged orders and convents had the right to be first served in all the public markets, and to take their choice of all the victuals there exposed. No layman had the right to make his day's market until the cooks of these favoured convents had first left the market-place. There were laws favouring the privileged castes, with special tribunals for their execution. Many public employments, judicial and administrative, were hereditary in the classes of the nobility, and of the Florentine and Sienese citizens. Personal merit, talent, and knowledge were in no account if the names of the parents were not to be found inscribed in the *Libri d'Ors*. All these public functionaries were poorly paid—in some cases not paid at all; the result being that they were venal, and often extortionate. The public expenditure was constantly in excess of the public income, and, of course, the treasury always drained. This state of matters provoked, under specious pretexts, extraordinary taxes and *voluntary* loans with promises of high interest and repayment which were never kept; redeemable and unredeemable forced loans, when the allurements and the promises of the voluntary loans had been held out in vain; an oppressive salt monopoly, a bread monopoly, an iron monopoly, and countless other monopolies; exclusive licenses granted for the retail trade of raw and manufactured materials—for the trade in the necessaries of human life, of domestic cattle. Nearly all the different sources of the public revenue not pledged for the payment of the interest of the public debt, farmed out to persons who grew rich by grinding down the wretched taxpayers to their last farthing." *

This miserable condition of affairs, deplorable as it was in the whole extent of the grand duchy, was marked by features of peculiar wretchedness in the province of Siena. And it was precisely in the province of Siena that, at the time when in France, the influence of Louis XIV.'s great protectionist Minister, Colbert, was all-paramount, and when in England financiers were out-Colberting Colbert in their insane protectionist rivalry, in the year 1677—three years after the death of Milton, and one year before the passing of the *habeas corpus* Act —there was born the economic sage, Sallustio Bandini, whose work, small in dimensions, but truly great by its wise thoughts and far-reaching influence, was destined to form so beneficent an epoch in the history of commercial liberty. This writer, in whose character and career one is at a loss what most to admire—whether his acuteness or his practical common sense, his philanthropy, his patriotism, his rare modesty, or his singular tenacity of will—was born of a noble family in Siena. Destined originally for the army, but showing a marked aversion to that career, he spent the first year of his manhood in the management of the family estates. Whilst thus employed, he acquired that intimate practical knowledge of the condition of the Sienese Maremma, and of the numerous and complicated causes of its misery, to which we owe his deep sympathy with the unhappy population, and the proposals of reformation

* *Zobi, "Manuale Storico,"* page 46.

embodied in his far-famed *Discorso Economico*. It was after a period of several years thus spent in the management of the Bandini estates that he resolved to enter the Church. He repaired to the university of Siena, after the requisite time took his degree as doctor of civil and canon law, and received holy orders: but, before settling down in his new profession in his native city of Siena, he determined to visit all the chief cities of Italy, and make the personal acquaintance of their most distinguished men. He repaired to and dwelt for some time, successively, in Naples, Rome, Bologna, Mantua, and Milan, bringing his course of travel to a close at the capital of his own state, Florence, in which last city he remained a considerable time. On his return to Siena, he was soon appointed one of the canons of the cathedral, then arch-priest, and finally archdeacon. A born reformer, he commenced his reforming efforts by proposing that the scholarships of the Siena university should be placed on a better footing, and awarded solely for merit—not merely through interest and favour. With the view of raising the standard of knowledge and education, then very low amongst the aspirants to holy orders—and, indeed, among the clergy themselves—he devoted the large income of his archdeaconry to the formation of a library, which was soon made by him to include the best works in profane as well as in sacred literature. This he presented, during his lifetime, to the university of Siena, appointing as curators the municipal council, and formally placing it under the protection of the grand duke. We are told of this extremely Broad Churchman that in the selection of the volumes he avoided as much as possible works tending to favour clerical encroachments on the rights of the State, and that no maxim was more frequently on his lips than the necessity for the clergy to enlarge and liberalise their ideas by a thorough acquaintance with the various branches of secular knowledge. .

B

Such was the enlightened and philanthropic eccle-
siastic who, towards the close of the Medicean dynasty,
conceived the idea of relieving the suffering of the
Sienese Maremma by repairing to Florence and submitting to the Grand Duke John Gaston his views
respecting the extent of a truly national calamity, and
his proposals for the mitigation of the same. He told
the sovereign that foremost among the causes by which
the Sienese Maremma was sinking down every day into
a state of greater misery were the improvident laws
by which the Sienese landed proprietors were prevented
in years of abundance from exporting their surplus produce. From the inability to dispose of the same in
foreign markets, they purposely let their fields grow
waste rather than incur the risk of adding new stores
of grain to harvests already superabundant, and thus
still more lowering the price of their produce in the
market. As kindred obstacles were thrown in the way
of importing grain, when such imports were most required, and as the very processes of reaping and storing
and selling were hampered by absurd regulations—as
a huge machinery of obstacles and difficulties clogged
in like manner the commercial action of the most common trades—the entire economic and commercial
system of the Sienese body politic had become vitiated,
and called for radical treatment and effectual cure.
What should be the first condition of that treatment,
and the first guarantee of that cure? The very easy
and simple method—such was Archdeacon Bandini's
reply—of leaving nature to itself; of allowing men to
buy and sell, according as the varying wants and
conditions of the market indicated. Grant complete
freedom to the corn trade; strike off the thousand
fetters by which the movements of home commerce
were impeded; instead of a cumbrous and costly system
of conveyances, by which the transfer of property was
rendered difficult and almost impossible, let contracts
be regulated by short, plain, and most clearly-expressed

laws—so clearly expressed as to be intelligible to all
ordinary capacities. On the true character and operation of a circulating medium the archdeacon's views
were not less precise. If you will only allow trade,
he said, to rest on a sounder and more natural footing,
so that money must constantly be changing hands,
you will have much less trouble about your currency.
It is with the circulation of a crown-piece as with the
rapid revolving of a lighted torch, which a boy keeps
whirling round and round. As he whirls it round
rapidly, the one point of light assumes the proportions
of a large unbroken circle of fire; and so the crown-
piece that in a single month passes through a hundred
hands possesses the value and does the work of a
hundred crowns. Such were the truths which Archdeacon Bandini sought to impress on the decrepit
Grand Duke John Gaston Medici and his councillors,
John Antonio Tornaquinci and Jacopo Giraldi. How
were these truths received? As the dreams of a
visionary—of one living in some ideal Utopia, instead
of that work-a-day Tuscan world which these practical
and practised statesmen were called upon to govern;
or rather as the ravings of a lunatic escaped from
Bedlam, whom, in the best interests of society, it was
imperative to seize and consign again to his straight-
waistcoat and his cell. Tornaquinci and Giraldi actually
proposed that the mad priest should be shut up in a
lunatic asylum; and if he escaped that fate, his escape
was owing partly to his age—for he was already about
sixty—partly to his character as a Churchman, and
partly to the fact of his belonging to a noble family,
and having very influential connections. Bandini did
not lose heart or hope. After his return to Siena he
passed his time in committing to writing the proposals
for the improvement of the Maremma which, with so
little success, and at such personal risk, he had laid
before the Grand Duke John Gaston. He composed
the celebrated "Economical Discourse;" and though

his lessons always remained in manuscript until several years after the writer's death, he had the satisfaction of knowing that they were appreciated by another and truly enlightened sovereign, the first grand duke of the new dynasty of Hapsburgh-Lorraine—the husband of ᵗhe Empress Maria Theresa—Francis II. For this early adoption of his views Bandini was indebted to the sincere friendship and enlightened patriotism of a comparatively young statesman, Pompeo Neri. Although the two Ministers of John Gaston, Tornaquinci and Giraldi, had treated him with such contempt, he had won the entire confidence of Neri, whose precocious talents, and, for his years, truly surprising erudition, had led to his appointment, at the age of twenty-one, as Professor of Public Law in the university of Pisa. Thence he had been called by the Grand Duke John Gaston to Florence, to share with his father, Neri Badia, the duties of auditor of the crown property. Whilst discharging the duties of this last office, Pompeo Neri, not yet thirty years of age, had the opportunity of learning, during Bandini's memorable visit to the court of Florence, all the wise proposals made by the philosophic archdeacon for the regeneration of the Sienese Maremma. In the mind of Pompeo Neri these truths, equally practical and philanthropic, found a congenial soil. They never ceased to colour his own long career of energetic and beneficent statesmanship; for he was destined to hold, at a later period, the first place in the councils of the Grand Duke Peter Leopold. But the first step in the realisation of Bandini's views followed on the presentation to the new Grand Duke Francis of the archdeacon by Pompeo Neri. Reserving to a later place in the narrative the detailed account of the manner in which, through Neri's initiative, these beneficent reforms were commenced, continued, and completed, it may suffice for the present to say that, in the story of the economic reform of Tuscany, under Peter Leopold, the two names of Sallustio Bandini and

Pompeo Neri hold, next to the name of the prince himself, the most conspicuous place. Had the noble-minded author of the " Economical Discourse" never pondered so deeply upon, and felt so keenly for, the desolate condition of the Sienese Maremma ; had he never urged his reforms so strongly on an ignorant, prejudiced, and scornful court ; the great work of economic progress in Tuscany, though sooner or later it might certainly have been effected, would, beyond all question, neither have begun so soon nor been carried out so thoroughly. Had the economic sage of Siena not found in Pompeo Neri so true a friend and so stout a backer, the march of reform, even though accepted in principle, would have sorely lagged in practice. Pompeo Neri was in truth one of the greatest statesmen of the eighteenth century, and he has left the impress of his genius not on Tuscany alone, but on all Italy. He had even stamped the impress of that genius during his lifetime on the Prussia of Frederick the Great. When, through the jealousy of rival ministers at Florence, he was trans-ferred for some years, by the wish of the Empress Maria Theresa, to the government of Milan, he succeeded in completely remodelling the whole municipal system of Lombardy ; and his plans for the valuation of all the landed property in the Lombard province excited at once the admiration and imitation of Frederick the Great, who made them the groundwork of a similar operation in Prussia, and, half a century later, com-manded the unqualified assent of Napoleon I., who caused them to be extended from Lombardy to the other parts of his kingdom of Italy. The annals of Tuscan economics offer to our view a group, numerous and varied, of far-seeing and patriotic statesmen, by whom the princes of Hapsburgh-Lorraine were aided in the prosecution of their generous task, and along with them, as their fellow-labourers, may be seen writers of no ordinary power. There is Richcourt, and Ginori, and

Rucellai ; there is the founder of the Georgofili
Montelatici, we have Pagnini and Tavanti, Paoletti and
Gianni, and Sarchiani ; there is Faproni ; and, though
last, not least, there is the great and the wise Vittorio
Fossombroni ; but far above the measure even of their
stature towers the colossal figure of Pompeo Neri. And
as we gaze upon him, we behold him towering above
a race of giants.

II.

WHEN Leibnitz, treating, two centuries ago, of the probable fortunes of Alsace and Lorraine, at a time when the national feeling of Germany was still smarting from their loss, mentally reviewed the various contingencies likely to arise from the same, he certainly anticipated a day when they would be reunited to the German Empire. But the very last thing of which he could possibly have dreamt was the fact that future dukes in name—for only in name were they sovereigns of Lorraine—should have their lives and memories associated with an economic catholicity quite as remarkable in its way as the projected union of different creeds and communions, to realise which the great German philosopher dedicated no slight portion of his life. We should be carried far beyond the limits and scope of this brief historical sketch by the attempt to narrate, in the most summary form, the varying tale of the international fiat which finally transferred the heritage of the extinct house of Medici to Duke Francis of Lorraine, the husband of the Empress Maria Theresa. That event occurred in 1737. The new ruler, on arriving in his Italian State, found a country financially impoverished and morally degraded. He remained but a short period at Florence, but before his return to Vienna left a regency to conduct the affairs of the Tuscan government. Of this regency the nominal head was the Prince de Craon, but its real chief, the guiding and controlling spirit of Tuscany during nearly the whole of the emperor grand duke's reign, was Count de Richcourt. By the side of Richcourt were other Ministers, the most remarkable being Neri and Rucellai.

The historic renown of the great Peter Leopold, the son and successor of Francis, has somewhat unduly and unfairly cast into the shade the sterling merits and real services of the regency by which Tuscany was ruled during his father's life. To the regency was due the initiative of nearly all the memorable reforms, for the thorough completion of which Peter Leopold's own reign has become so deservedly renowned. The Grand Duke Francis had scarcely arrived in Florence when, as was already mentioned, Pompeo Neri presented to the new sovereign his friend Sallustio Bandini. The Archdeacon of Siena testified his loyalty to the prince and his love for his fellow-subjects by offering to the Grand Duke Francis the manuscript of his "Economical Discourse." The grand duke studied carefully its contents, and was so much struck with the truth and soundness of the reasoning that he determined to lose no time in giving effect to the archdeacon's proposals. He issued an edict by which the landowners of the Sienese Maremma were at once empowered to export two-thirds of all the corn grown in the country. The edict was to remain in force for a period of twelve years. But this temporary and tentative character was merely apparent ; at the end of the twelve years the edict was renewed ; a second renewal occurred after the lapse of another twelve years, until at length the provisions applicable at first only to the Sienese Maremma were embodied in the general legislation of the State.

The grand duchy was at that time divided into two quite separate governments—the administration of Florence, with the provinces immediately dependent, being quite separate from the administration of Siena ; and the Florence authorities, with whose acts in this matter the Grand Duke Francis did not interfere, regarded a Free Trade in cereals from a point of view exactly the reverse of that from which it was beheld by Bandini, Neri, and the sovereign himself. The Grand Duke Francis had scarcely left Florence to return to Vienna when the

Florence magistrates of "Abundance," the *Abbondanza*
—the department would have been much more fitly
designated one for the creation of scarcity than of
abundance—fulminated decrees of a perfectly ferocious
character against the malefactors who should dare to
export grain from the State. They were to be consigned
to the galleys, their property was to be confiscated ;
though native Florentines, in consideration of their
citizenship, were treated with less rigour, and con-
signed to the city prisons instead of being sentenced
to hard labour in the galleys. Free Trade in Tuscany has had its precursor saints and its great apostles ;
if we are not equally familiar with the names of its con-
fessors and its martyrs, we are at least left in no doubt
about the supreme enactments which rendered the con-
fession hazardous, and the martyrdom secure.

The first serious financial problem with which the
new government had to deal presented itself in connection with the exceptional privileges of the clergy. More
than half the real property of the whole state was in the
hands of the Church ; the income of the clergy in 1737
much exceeded the revenues of the State, which, at that
time, from all the various sources, including even the
private property of the Crown, was not more than
1,214,000 Tuscan crowns. In a population of about
900,000 souls the ecclesiastics of all conditions, the
secular and regular clergy, and the nuns, amounted to
27,108 persons. In this number the nuns are separately
given at 9,584. From the above figures it will be seen
that every thirty-second person in the State was a priest,
a monk, or a nun. Thus a class amounting numerically
to the thirty-second part of the population owned more
than half the property of the country, and this class, as
was stated above, paid no taxes, direct or indirect,
ordinary or extraordinary. The first great financial measure of the new government made known its
resolution to place the clergy on the same footing
with all other classes of citizens, to make them, like

those other classes, contribute their fair share of the public burdens. In connection with the proposed dynastic changes and political arrangements which led finally to the accession of the House of Hapsburgh-Lorraine, Spanish garrisons had been occupying different points of the grand duchy. To meet the expenses arising from these garrisons a special tax was imposed, and the clergy were called upon to make a declaration of their revenues, for the purpose of fixing the quota which they must pay. The clergy objected to paying anything ; they stood on their privileges ; they appealed to Rome. In this general mutiny there was, as might have been expected, one memorable exception. Sallustio Bandini urged upon his reverend brethren the common duty of sharing the burdens of the State, the common protector ; but it was all to no purpose. It might have been supposed that, as the reigning pontiff, Clement XII., of the Corsini family, was a Tuscan, the sovereign of Tuscany might have found it easier to come to terms with the Holy See. Clement XII., however, was strongly imbued with the maxims of the Roman Curia. But in his successor, Prospero Lambertina, of Bologna, who, three years later, took possession of the Papal chair under the title of Benedict XIV., the reforming princes of the House of Hapsburgh-Lorraine had the rare fortune of always dealing with a pontiff of singular conscientiousness, moderation, and Christian charity. No amount of zeal for his order, or for the privileges of his high office, ever prevented Benedict XIV. from submitting to the most candid examination the views of others, or to the most severe examination his own plans and purposes ; and though conflicts and collisions were constantly arising between the Tuscan clergy and the Tuscan Government, they certainly neither originated in, nor were embittered by, the action of the pontiff. The lay and clerical powers looked at the same question, as may well be supposed, from extremely different points of view. The lay government was resolved that the economic progress of the State should not be arrested by the special privileges of the clergy ; the spiritual power thought itself bound to maintain and uphold its inherited rights and privileges ; the contest was always carried on, but it would be difficult to name any European State of the eighteenth century where it was conducted in a fairer spirit than between the Tuscan Regency, under the Grand Duke Francis II., and Prospero Lambertini.

In this first passage of arms between the Roman Curia and the Tuscan Government, occasioned by the tax for the Spanish garrisons, the remonstrances and protests of the Curia were disregarded. The actual sum obtained was in itself but a small matter, but the principle involved was one of enormous, incalculable magnitude ; and in the resolution and consistency with which that principle was enforced, an attentive observer might clearly have descried the commencement of a new and a better state of things.

It may be worth while at this place to state briefly the problem which the new government had before it, and the very imperfect means at its command for making out the same. In the first place, it found the old commercial traditions of Florence rather a hindrance than a help. Such Tuscans as thought at all upon the subject, not unnaturally believed that the same causes which had contributed to the past, might call into existence a future greatness of their country. They had once been great through trade and manufactures ; why might they not by the same means become great again ? They had regarded agriculture with contempt ; why should they now look to that quarter for hope or help ? The first difficulty of the new government—and it was no common difficulty—lay in the necessity that the national mind should be disabused of these two kindred prejudices. Manufacturing and commercial superiority had, through an infinite variety of causes, become transferred from Florence to Holland and to England ; in a less degree to

other countries.   But the agricultural resources of the
Tuscan State were quite undeveloped, and might, through
proper management, yield plenty and prosperity to this
population of less than a million souls.   In order, however, to attain this result, physical, political, legal, social,
religious difficulties had to be overcome.   The broad
tracts of land in which corn could be grown must first
be rendered habitable for human beings.   The tillers of
the soil must be preserved from the pestilential fevers by
which wide districts were continually scourged.   Then
a political system of long standing, by which Siena
had ever been treated as a conquered province, had to
be overthrown.   Nay, more ; the entire political organisation of society—the system by which great properties,
in virtue of the entails, were massed in the hands of
a few proprietors, had to be broken up.   That wide-
stretching legal network of useless and expensive, often
most irrational and unjust, forms, had to be torn in
pieces. A system of social conventionalities, deliberately
built up by the princes of the house of Medici, with
the view of casting discredit on habits of self-help, of
individual energy, of honest, sturdy labour, for the
purpose of throwing a prestige around the crawling
courtiers who swarmed in the Pitti Palace ; this system
of social conventionalities had to be dashed in pieces
and scattered to the winds.   And religious prejudices,
of which the roots had for centuries struck deep in the
soil of European life; religious influences which again and
again had, during these centuries, successfully confronted
the mightiest princes ; time-honoured "religious orders,"
long accustomed to act with the regularity and disci-
pline of well-trained Janizaries, by commands received
from Rome—all these had to be faced and fought
against, if the work was ever to be achieved.   And this
work, it must likewise be remembered, was the self-
chosen task of a petty Italian State—of one small in
comparison even with the other States of the Italian
peninsula, to say nothing of the great military monarchies

of Europe. It proposed to enter on a course of civil and economic reform without being deterred by the thought that at any moment it might be whirled into the general vortex of European politics, even when that vortex might assume the most warlike form. The ancient proverb, declaring that little men should not wear large shoes, was altogether disregarded by this petty State. We shall find—and in making the discovery a pitying smile involuntarily mingles with our admiration—that this first, this model Free Trade State of Europe, proclaims in the tone of Frederick or Catherine, with a dignity befitting the elder Pitt, "that the first principle of its policy is to preserve perpetual neutrality amidst the surging strife of European animosity and war!"

There exists no full and reliable account, either by contemporary or later writers, of the internal state of Tuscany, its population and resources, under the Regency. We have, however, two documents written about the same period—1757—by the examination and comparison of which a certain degree of insight may be gained. The first is a short memoir by Angelo Tavanti, the secretary of finance, or chancellor of the exchequer, of the Regency, written for the purpose of determining as nearly as possible the amount of money in circulation. For English readers the short but most suggestive and admirably-reasoned paper of Tavanti has a peculiar interest, showing as it does the perfect familiarity of these Tuscan economists and statesmen with the doctrines of Sir William Petty, of Locke, and of Hume. Smith's "Wealth of Nations," it is almost needless to remark, was not published until nineteen years later. Tuscany, remarks Tavanti, has a population of little less than nine hundred thousand souls. Of this population, it is estimated that two-thirds are engaged in agricultural pursuits. The value of the agricultural produce may therefore be deduced as follows :—A Tuscan peasant cannot be fed, clothed, keep his spades, ploughs, hoes, &c., in order, and pay his quota of the public taxes, for less than twenty crowns a year. Now, assuming that the number of peasants is five hundred and fifty thousand, that will give a sum of eleven million Tuscan crowns annually. As the peasants have only about half the value of the entire produce, another eleven millions of crowns may be placed to the account of the landowners. Assuming, then, the truth of Hume's principle, that the money required for the circulating medium of a country ought to be about a third of the annual value of the rent received by the landowner, one may fairly conclude that the money circulating in Tuscany cannot be much less than 3,666,666 crowns. Nearly the same result, says Tavanti, will be obtained on Locke's theory. Locke holds that the circulating medium of a State in a normal condition of traffic should equal a fourth of the rents paid to the landowner—in other words, to the fiftieth part of the wages of the working classes, and to the twentieth part of the general value of the commission and retail trades. Starting from this principle, the fourth part of the collective rental of eleven millions would be 2,750,000. If, again, we take the population of the working classes, of all engaged in trades and manufacture, at a hundred and sixty thousand, and assume that the average gain of each is fifty crowns a year, the collective amount will be eight millions annually, and the sum paid every week for wages will be a hundred and sixty thousand crowns. The commission, trade, &c., cannot be reckoned at less than twelve millions a year, of which the twentieth part would be a hundred and sixty thousand crowns, giving altogether 3,513,000 crowns. A still clearer process may be employed. Assuming that the entire raw and manufactured produce of Tuscany is just about equal to the wants of the inhabitants, and that the surplus exchangeable for foreign goods is such that the general wealth of the country is neither increasing nor diminishing in any very sensible degree, the following further conclusions may be drawn :—Agricultural produce, it has been seen, may be reckoned at twenty-two millions of crowns. The value of Tuscan manufactures may be calculated at eight millions more. There is thus a total of thirty millions of crowns. Tavanti then goes into details on the proportions, whether of money or kind, in which the peasant receives his wages, or the owner obtains his rent. The value of the wages or the rent in kind may be estimated at sixteen millions, and twenty millions would be required in the requisite money transactions for that amount. If the money in circulation changed hands four times a year, only five millions would be required ; if six times, only 3,333,333 crowns. But taking as the safest hypothesis that the money changed hands five times a year, the amount of circulating medium required would be four millions.

In the same year in which Tavanti submitted these calculations to the government, an intelligent Lombard nobleman, Count Carli, at that time residing in Tuscany, endeavoured to form an estimate, which was not published until thirty years later, of the general extent of Tuscan trade, of the exports and imports. On the first head, he was so fortunate as to obtain a tolerably detailed account from Gianni, then at the head of the Pisan custom-house, and afterwards one of the ablest and most useful Ministers of Peter Leopold. According to the data furnished by Gianni, Tuscany exported annually to the amount of 1,268,000 Tuscan crowns. Of this sum, 469,000 must be set down to the account of vegetable and animal produce. In the much larger sum representing manufactures, 700,000 crowns are given as the value of the Tuscan silks, and 20,000 crowns as that of Leghorn straw bonnets. Of the agricultural produce then exported, cereals, &c., figure at 60,000 crowns, wine at 75,000 crowns, and oil at 80,000 crowns. Though Count Carli did not obtain the details of the imports, as of the exports, he was led to believe that the value of the two was nearly equal.

If to the data thus furnished by Tavanti on the population of the State the relative proportion of the same employed in agricultural or other pursuits, the rate at which they lived, and the money which they required to carry on business; if to the further data supplied by Count Carli on the value of exports and imports we add the amount of the public debt, the sum drawn chiefly from the land-tax, required to pay the interest of the same, and the sum derived from all other sources of revenue which the tax-collectors, to whom the taxes had been farmed out, paid into the government treasury, we shall obtain about as correct an idea of the commercial and financial state of Tuscany under the Regency as it is possible now to get. The public debt, taking its rise in the successive loans contracted by the Republic and the grand dukes of the house of Medici, amounted, at the time when the first sovereign of Hapsburgh-Lorraine ascended the throne, to 14,250,000 Tuscan crowns. As the annual interest of this debt, the loans being nearly all at five per cent., was defrayed from the land-tax, we may assume that 712,500 crowns, with the further expenses of collection, was obtained from that source. The sum obtained from other sources, and paid over by the farmers-general of the taxes to the treasury, under three or four other quite insignificant heads, amounted to 933,298 crowns. These last data are given from the returns of 1758—therefore only a year later than the notices furnished by Tavanti and Carli. Putting these various facts together, we may form a rough estimate of Tuscan trade and finances in 1777-78—twenty years after the accession of the Grand Duke Francis II. There had already been progress. The tide had turned as regards population—instead of a constant decrease, there was an increase. If economical progress was slow, the difficulty arose in great part from that very system of farming out the revenues of the State which had been decreed by the Emperor Grand Duke Francis at Vienna, without consulting his Tuscan minister, almost at the commencement of his reign. This improvident and in many different ways most hurtful measure had been occasioned by the necessity of pledging the public credit of Tuscany in order to raise a loan asked by the Empress Maria Theresa from her husband, with a view of meeting in part the expenses of the War of Succession.

There is yet a fourth document of the same year's date— 1757—which might usefully be studied in connection with the three papers quoted above. It supplies us with the probable estimates of the following year. Some of the items are sufficiently curious. Thus, the sum set down for all the salaries, &c., of the Ministry of Finance, only exceeds the sum required for the grand-ducal liveries by a very small amount. Still, the document, however suggestive in showing how the public money was spent, belongs rather to the history of public administration than to a narrative professing first and chiefly to deal with national economics.

A threefold misfortune was entailed on the country through the arrangements connected with this measure— namely, the loan made by the Grand Duke Francis to his wife, Maria Theresa. One extremely bad result was the justification, based on fiscal necessities, which it was supposed to give for the establishment of State lotteries. Lotteries had been prohibited by the last grand duke of the house of Medici. The prohibition was renewed by Prince de Craon, as head of the regency, on the accession of Francis II. But the supposed necessities of the revenue were too imperious, and the public lottery offices were soon in full force. The second evil, caused by the farming-out of the taxes to a private company, was the frightful amount of hardship and extortion practised by the swarm of the company's agents, the sub-contractors. Against their misdeeds there was no remedy, because the court to which appeals could be made was, in

C

reality, nominated by the company itself. But in its direct bearings on the progress of commercial liberty, the worst of all the evils was the following. The State Taxation Company, if we may so term it, having once made its arrangements with the various departments of customs, excise, with the registration and post-offices, with the separate heads of salt, tobacco, and spirit monopolies, with the land-conveyance and baronial fief office, naturally enough regarded the conservation of the whole system from which its profits were derived as a matter of life and death. It was up in arms on every attempt to introduce financial or commercial reforms by which it would be the loser. If it was proposed to reduce the public burdens, and meet many of the State expenses by the sale of the vast crown-lands formerly belonging to the house of Medici, the State Taxation Company, represented successively by MM. Lambart, Masson, Diodati, Guadagni, Martelli, and Seristori, did everything in its power to frustrate so beneficial a measure. If Pompeo Neri represented to his colleagues in the administration of the regency that commercially it was a great mistake for a bale of wool when sent only from Leghorn to Cortona to be stopped during the transit at ten separate custom-houses, and pay local duties under forty-four different heads, the State Taxation Company would answer that in fine-spun economic theories Pompeo Neri's objections might be all very true, but that if the State Taxation Company did not receive from these different custom-houses the sums stipulated by contract, it could not undertake to send to Vienna the four hundred thousand Tuscan crowns annually transmitted to His Majesty the Emperor Grand-Duke. Thus the really enlightened legislative and administrative acts of the regency were constantly rendered inoperative through the selfish and interested opposition of the State Taxation Company; and its influence had become so notoriously and undeniably hurtful that one of the first acts of Peter Leopold's government was, by the advice of Neri, to annul, though at a very large pecuniary sacrifice, the contracts, and thus to leave the State in the complete possession of its financial and economic liberty.

It is easy to understand how the action of such a company, hurtful everywhere, must have proved exceptionally detrimental in the province of Siena, and how the seventy-thousand Tuscan crowns which it paid annually into the treasury from Siena represented—even more there than it would have done elsewhere—an amount of wrong-headedness, of commercial blundering, of agricultural stagnation, of administrative and judicial delay, most calamitous. The right freely to export corn was a great boon. But even for the exportation of corn there is one condition preceding and predominating all other conditions—that the human agents employed in the production of corn shall possess health and strength ; that their work shall not be constantly carried on under circumstances a hundred times more threatening to life than the chances of explosion in any carefully conducted gunpowder manufactory. It is but too certain that in the Sienese Maremma, under the regency which governed for the Emperor Grand-Duke Francis, this condition was not complied with. The official reports from the province at that time narrate, as quite an ordinary occurrence, how the fever-stricken peasants fell down exhausted in the fields or on the highways ; how they expired on the spot where they fell ; and how the dead bodies were left to rot because no hand of a fellow-man removed and buried them. And the same official reports tell how, even when buried, matters were no better, because the tombs in so many country churches were without a covering, and the festering corpses made the attendance at divine worship about as dangerous as the attendance in a typhus hospital. The same official reports tell us how, of a thousand labourers brought as colonists from Lorraine, and settled in the two spots of Sovana and Massa, there remained in life only thirty-five—three in the first and thirty-two in the second place.

The administration of the regency did what it could. It proposed wise laws. It procured—though, from the residence of the emperor grand-duke at Vienna, this was not done without much delay—the sanction of the sovereign to the same. It sought to put them in execution, though in doing so it had to contend against various and powerful opponents—the clergy, the nobility, the State Taxation Company. It was often hampered by the insubordination of its own officials, and even by the jealousy and rivalry amongst its own members. Count Richcourt, the real head of the government, was, as we have seen, jealous of Neri, and never rested until he got him removed to Milan. The Marquis Carlo Ginori, the Governor of Leghorn, was jealous of Richcourt, and never rested until he got him removed to Vienna. Their common task might, from its very nature, have suggested the necessity of unity and harmony of action. In the attempt to develop the national resources, the first thing required was, so far as possible, to transfer the property of the soil from idle and unproductive to active and productive hands. This at once involved the necessity of passing such laws as might arrest the further accumulation of property by the regular and secular clergy. The returns of 1750 gave the value of Church property at 25,000,000 Tuscan crowns. By a law, of which it is impossible to overrate the importance, promulgated in Vienna on the 1st of February of the following year, all religious bodies were prohibited from acquiring additional property. Legacies for masses and charitable purposes, but not exceeding two hundred Tuscan crowns, formed the sole exception to the sweeping provisions of this law. It prepared the way for still more comprehensive enactments in the reign of Peter Leopold.

A similar preparation for subsequent Leopoldine

laws equally or even more affecting the conditions of
land tenure is to be found in the law of 22nd June,
1747, by which the emperor grand-duke restricted the
right of creating entails, and determined the conditions
under which the existing entails might in many cases
be brought to a close. The measure was evidently of
a tentative and transitional character. For the present
it restricted the heirs of entail to four generations or
degrees. It accorded the right of creating new entails
only to nobles, and the property must be funded, not
landed. The second of these conditions involved the
very awkward and difficult question, what Tuscan
families had really the right to be considered noble.
No wonder if the herald's college at Florence presented
the spectacle of a furious battle-field, on which the
descendants of the old barons of the German Empire,
of the knights created by the Florentine Republic, and
of the marquises and counts ennobled for very equivocal
services by the princes of the house of Medici, fought
desperately for their family trees and armorial bearings.
The legislation of the regency, and in a much higher
degree that of Peter Leopold, were constantly combating deep-rooted social prejudices injurious to habits
of self-help and true economic progress. They seemed
never tired of repeating that every member of society
must be useful as well as ornamental. *Noblesse oblige*
is ever in the preambles of their laws. The "Corinthian
capitals of society" are reminded that their elegance
must not be disunited from solidity and strength. This
feeling is the key to not a few enactments which would
otherwise seem pedantic and intermeddling. The lawgiver sets his face against the extravagance of funerals,
because money may be more profitably spent in helping
the living than in lavishing costly and ostentatious
tributes to the dead. Then, as the number of civil and
religious holidays involved an immense loss of time
and labour to all classes, the regency at once abolished
all the civil festivals established by the Medici to com-

memorate their dynastic triumphs, and entered into
negotiations with Rome, which the good sense and
justice of Benedict XIV. soon brought to a successful
issue, and by which twenty-one Church holidays were
rendered no longer obligatory, and a number of half-
holidays practically abolished. By the operation of
these last laws, at least six weeks in the year were
added to the time available for labour. The regency,
it was true, established certain legal holidays of its own,
but the measure had the express scope of facilitating
rural labour. It advised the sovereign to promulgate
a law by which no writ could be served on the
persons engaged in agricultural labour during the
first half of July, the ordinary season of the Tuscan
harvest.

In 1763, just as the regency was drawing to its
close, a group of capitalists whose proposals were sup-
ported, drawn up in an official form, and most luminously
commented on, by Pompeo Neri, offered to take the
entire Sienese Maremma into their hands, and to
execute the great sanitary, hydraulic, and agricultural
operations necessary for its regeneration. The twenty-
six articles of their proposed charter, read by the light
of Neri's illustration, are nothing less than a most valuable contribution to political science. The writer appears
to have had the constitution and working of the East
India Company chiefly before his eyes. In dealing with
the Maremma, he says, we have no mere question of
commercial and agricultural progress. A country has to
be peopled, and the peopling of a country is a problem
of government in the widest sense of the word. All
political forces, civil, criminal, military, judicial, must be
made to converge, if we are to expect a favourable result.
Neri, therefore, proposes that his company shall be armed
with as ample powers as those possessed by the East
India Company, or by any of the Dutch or French
colonists. One has only to read the fifth article of the

proposed charter—that conferring on the company the full right to deal with the troublesome feudal lords of the Sienese Maremma—and to weigh all the reasons alleged by Neri for its necessity, in order clearly to understand why the mere passing of a law granting to the corn-growers of the Sienese Maremma the right of freely exporting their grain was by itself a most inadequate remedy for a vast amount of economic and social wretchedness.

Neri's plans appeared to have obtained no favour in the eyes of Marshal Botta Adorna, the chief person in the government of the regency towards its close, and according to all contemporary testimony one of the most incapable and worthless politicians of his time. The misplaced favour of the Emperor Grand-Duke Francis had placed him at the head of the Tuscan Government, after the death of the two most prominent Tuscan states-men. The Marquis Carlo Ginori had procured the transference of Count Richcourt to what in appearance was a higher post at Vienna. But Richcourt quite understood the real meaning of his being "kicked up-stairs" into the Aulic Council. A fit of apoplexy, brought on by excess of mortification at his fall, con-signed him to the tomb. Another fit of apoplexy, brought on by excess of exultation at his rise, struck down the triumphant rival, Carlo Ginori. The ancients would have held that an implacable because unpropitiated Nemesis had so aimed its shaft at the one as to cause it to glance off and deal a second death-blow on the person of the other. Death, indeed, was now the great actor on the stage of Tuscan politics. On the evening of the 18th of August, 1765, at Innspruck, amongst the festivities for the marriage of the Archduke Peter Leopold with the Infanta Maria Luisa of Spain, the Emperor Grand-Duke Francis, after leaving the theatre, shared the fate of his two ministers, and was, in his turn, struck dead by a fit of apoplexy. But death was raging with unwonted fury in hamlets and hovels, as well as palaces. In the first months of 1764 Tuscany was scourged by a famine, which in the history of Tuscan commercial legislation plays a part not inferior to that performed by the Irish potato-famine in the abolition of the English corn-laws.

III.

WHEN the Emperor Grand-Duke Francis II. died, he was followed to the grave by the gratitude, the blessings, and the sorrow of the Tuscan people. Though an absentee sovereign, his conduct during the last two years of his reign had especially endeared him to the great mass of his subjects. The natural benevolence of his character had shone forth with surprising brightness in the great famine of 1763-4. For a long time the country, even with its experience of Maremma scarcity, had not been doomed to witness such a calamity in such terrible proportions. The incessant rains of 1763 had utterly destroyed the crops. The Protectionist principles dominant at Florence in the administrative department, termed with such cruel irony that of *Abbondanza*, consistent in their logic, no more allowed the importation of foreign than the exportation of native corn. We have seen at a previous stage of the narrative how, when the exportation of grain was legalised in the Sienese Maremma, the proposal only called forth fresh penal enactments of unusual rigour from the Protectionist *Abbondanza* at Florence. And now the value of that Protectionist system was to be subjected to a frightful test. As the autumn and winter drew on, the scanty supplies of food, the surplus of the previous year, rapidly diminished. In the February of 1764 these scanty supplies had quite run out. But long before matters had reached this point the famine had begun, and was sternly carrying on its work. After the old, and the feeble, and the children had been killed off, amid such attempts as we read about in the siege of Jerusalem by Titus, the attempts to prolong existence by devouring ravenously garbage and offal, one saw bands of gaunt wolfish beings prowling over the land, seeking to rob from those still possessing a small stock of food what might satisfy the cravings of their own hunger. If the streets of the towns did not exhibit the same reckless violence, they were not the less echoing all day, and through the long night, with the cries of the famished sufferers. Then with the spring of 1764 came the general fever, the sure consequence of the general famine, &c. In this state of matters the head of the regency, Marshal Botta Adorna, proposed to the Emperor Grand-Duke his remedial measures. They consisted in the imposition of a new and heavy tax on the whole country, in the purchase by the government of foreign corn whilst the famine was at its height, and in closing all the ports against that foreign corn as soon as such a course might be considered practical. The *Abbondanza*, through whose officers alone foreign corn could be legally purchased, backed Marshal Botta Adorna's proposal. A proposal of a very different kind was transmitted to the Emperor Grand-Duke at Vienna by Pompeo Neri. Neri informed his sovereign that, in the economical state of the country, the attempt to impose any new tax must produce results much akin to the process of putting out a fire by pumping oil upon the flames. Rather let the Tuscan ports be entirely thrown open to the foreign corn trade. If this were done, and accompanied by a complete removal, not merely of the duty payable when the corn entered the country, but of all the duties payable in the interior at the various local custom-houses, if this wise and more rational course were taken, the effects of the calamity would soon be lessened. Neri's proposals encountered the fiercest opposition from Botta-Adorna and the *Abbondanza*. But the heart equally with the head of the Emperor Grand-Duke was on the side of Neri. In his reply he said, " New taxes must not be so much as spoken of ; I insist that such a proposal shall not be again transmitted to me. At such a crisis as this it is my duty to share as far as I can the trials of my subjects, not to increase them by new burdens. I therefore order that from my own private treasury the suffering shall be relieved as far as possible ; that, in addition to the gratuitous help, such advances of money as may be made shall be given free of interest." Help now became possible. With the opening of the ports, with the removal of the frontier and internal duties, corn poured in from abroad ; and in the month of June, 1764, the food, which four months previously no sum could purchase, was to be had all over the grand duchy at its normal price.

Mr. Cobden, when addressing the Academy of Georgofili, in Florence, on the 2nd of May, 1847, remarked : —"The chief cause that immediately and directly brought about the abolition of the English corn-laws might be termed a mere accident—the Irish potato famine. The service of my fellow-labourers and myself was to have so prepared the public mind, that it became possible to take advantage of that accident. But then," the speaker hastened to add, "one should bear in mind that such accidents, in the course of history, almost always turn to the account of reason and of justice." It may with equal truth be said that the accident of the great Tuscan famine of 1763-4 played the chief part in the abolition of the old Tuscan corn-laws ; but that result would never have been obtained if the minds of those to whom the destinies of the Tuscan State were entrusted had not been first prepared by Salustio Bandini and Pompeo Neri to take advantage of its tremendous lessons. The new sovereign, for the Grand Duke Peter Leopold, on his accession to the throne, had not reached the age of twenty, accorded his entire confidence to Pompeo Neri. A natural respect for the wishes of his mother, the Empress Maria Theresa, prevented him from dismissing at once the head of the late regency—Marshal Botta Adorna. The same feeling of respect induced him to place, but to keep only for a short time, at the head of the government Count Orsini de Rosemberg. But the most influential member of the cabinet was Pompéo Neri, who managed the home department, and before long he became the official and, recognised as he had already been, the real premier. Neri appears to have lost no time in thoroughly indoctrinating the young grand duke in Free-Trade principles; and the opportunity of putting them in force very soon presented itself, for another "accident"—a second famine, caused by the failing crops of 1766—seemed to menace Tuscany, and, if one judged from the utter ruin of the harvest, in more alarming proportions than the calamity by which the land had been scourged three years before. But the first great dearth had, at any rate, left behind its compensating and remedial moral. Pompeo Neri set forth to the young prince the means by which the evil had been arrested, and with the view, not merely of providing against another temporary misfortune, but of permanently placing the cereal supplies of the State on a sound and rational basis, he proposed that a complete freedom of trade in corn should be made one of the fundamental laws of the State. It required no little prudence and tact to bring this about. All the class interests opposed to the change were up in arms. The functionaries of the *Abbondanza* saw their occupation gone. The Tuscan landowners were, of course, terrified at the prospect of the diminished value of their harvests. The State Taxation Company and all the government officials connected with the internal custom-houses dreaded a measure which would no longer furnish them with an opportunity of procuring a common gain. The patented and privileged corn-merchants, the patented and privileged bakers—for without a special privilege no man had the right to bake a loaf of bread—predicted that the change must reduce all Tuscany to a state of absolute starvation. The agitators and intriguers of Protectionism worked on the ignorance and fears of the poorer classes. " Bread! bread! we want bread, not laws!" was the cry of the misguided mobs. But the youthful prince stood firmly by his great minister. By two laws, of 6th August and 15th September, 1766, he gave the death-blow to the Tuscan corn-laws. The first of these two enactments removed the duty on foreign corn. The second measure removed all obstacles to the free circulation of corn in the interior of the State, suspended all the exclusive privileges for the making and sale of bread, and prohibited the officials of the *Abbondanza*, and the kindred departments hitherto charged with the regulation of food supplies, from any further intermeddling in the matter.

Although the deficiency in the Tuscan harvest of 1766 was really much greater than that of 1763, its calamitous effects, just because remedial steps were taken in time, bore no comparison to those of the previous famine. Such, however, was the strength of the class interests, that in some parts of the country the subordinate local authorities refused to carry out the provisions of the two laws. Their opposition only served to make Peter Leopold more determined to prosecute the Free-Trade policy which he had begun. He ordered that the question should be discussed in the Council of Ministers in the comprehensive form, whether the entire and absolute liberty of the corn trade was adapted to the condition of Tuscany. In the discussion thus provoked Neri passed in review the entire commercial and agricultural position of the State. He combated the popular belief that the future of Tuscany lay in a return to the manufacturing greatness by which Florence was so wealthy and so famous in the days of the Republic. Commercial supremacy had, he declared, passed away to other countries—to England, to Holland. The chief heritage bequeathed by the entire manufacturing system of the Florentine Republic was one which ought to be got rid of as soon as possible —a complicated, and cumbersome, and most embarras-

sing mass of trade regulations and bye-laws, having
only one effect, that of preventing Tuscan trades and
manufactures from making even the comparative small
improvement which it might be now in their power to
realise.   Tuscany should now concentrate its energies
on the development of its agricultural resources.   "The
complete freedom of the corn trade," he remarked,
"which, of course, must prove the principal means of
augmenting the quantity of this article and its value—
this article being the most important production of our
soil, and consequently our chief source of income—this
complete freedom should be accepted as the fundamental
basis of our economic laws.   In a State which recognises
no other source of subsistence save the produce of its
land, it is impossible to subject the most important
form of this produce to regulations which either limit
its value or cut off at any moment the possibility of
finding the equivalent fruits of the labourer, or of those
who undertake great labours with the scope of investing
the profits in new cultivations.   Such restrictions necessarily create the great injury of bringing about a consequent diminution of produce."   Neri traced the first
origin of the restrictions in the trade of corn to the
provisions in the old Roman laws, and he combated the
popular prejudices ; indeed, from the part played in
the same by mistaken religious views, they might be
termed superstitious, by which the trade in corn, and
the accumulation of that article, were made the subject
of severe penal laws.
    The arguments advanced by Neri in the minis-
terial discussions have been embodied by him in the
memoir published in the Appendix to the Chevalier
Fabbroni's work, the "Provvedimenti Annonari."   Next
to the celebrated discourse of his master and friend
Bandini, this memoir of Neri is, beyond all question,
the most important monument, both in the special
history of Tuscan, and in the general history of
Italian Free Trade.   It is only justice to the memory

of this great statesman to give the due prominence to the part which he at this time played in the councils of Peter Leopold, and in the regeneration of the Tuscan State. When he and his two fellow-labourers, Tavanti and Rucellai, disappeared from the scene, the work of reform was not prosecuted, towards the close of Peter Leopold's reign, with the same energy by which the commencement had been marked. Not that, if we except one really amusing instance, Protectionist principles or practice ever came into vogue. The sound maxims of Free Trade were steadily professed in the highest quarters ; but there was wanting the quick eye and the firm hand which had previously caused all the subordinate functionaries to act in harmony with the impulse given from above. To revert, however, to the period of the great corn-law reform, the work kept steadily advancing. A more comprehensive law, of the 18th September, 1767, swept away definitively all taxes, and patents, and privileges impeding the making or the sale of bread. All duties on the importation of foreign corn were removed. The merely nominal restrictions— for they were nothing more, in virtue of which the importation could begin to take effect only when home-grown corn rose in the market above a certain price—fourteen Tuscan lire the sack—did not long continue to hold their place in the statute book. These restrictions, too, were completely removed by the later law of the 25th February, 1771 ; and a final edict of the 24th August, 1775, decreed the abolition of the " congregation of the Annona, and of all the other offices established for the purpose of regulating the introduction into the country, the manufacture, the sale, and the transit of grain and bread." Henceforth the trade in cereals in all its forms, native and foreign, and with all its consequences, became completely free. It was an appropriate termination of this work that at this epoch of his reign Peter Leopold gave orders that the economic discourse of Bandini, which had hitherto remained in manuscript, should be printed at the grand-ducal printing-office, and given to the world as the scientific justification of the policy which he was pursuing.

The writer of a Cobden Club essay will scarcely, one may assume, be required by its readers to offer any special demonstration of the wisdom and justice revealed in the policy of the Tuscan reformer, or to dwell on the truth that complete freedom of trade in the first necessary of life is the primary and indispensable condition for the development of all other phases of commercial liberty. Yet in recording the fact that Tuscany was the first civilised State to profess and, except when disturbed by foreign influences, constantly to act upon this policy, it may be worth while to bear in mind the manifold civilising consequences bound up with the same. Tuscany has enjoyed the inestimable blessing of obtaining during a whole century the food of its population at the lowest price quoted in the regular returns of the European markets. Now unless social science and statistical inquiry have all been working in vain, a minimum of food prices means—other conditions being equal—a maximum of provident marriages amongst rural labourers and artisans; it means a minimum in those habits of female profligacy which are more directly traceable to domestic poverty and wretchedness; it means a minimum in offences against property and person so far as they spring from the same cause; it means a minimum of temptations to agitation and revolution, and in that direction a maximum of security to public order and national credit. In the memorable speech, already quoted, which Mr. Cobden addressed to the Florence Academy of the Georgofili on the 2nd of May, 1847, he said:—" I have always preferred to look at the moral rather than at the material aspects of free trade. Not that I despise the accumulation of wealth, which means, in other words, the multiplication of the conveniences, of the facilities, and the greater diffusion of civilisation. But political economy means more than a treatise on the wealth of nations; it means justice practised between man and man on the greatest possible scale. Free Trade has a yet loftier mission than the exchange of wares between different nations; it tends to remove prejudices of birth, of colour, of religion, and of race, and to unite the human family by the bonds of brotherhood and of interdependency." In these noble words we recognise what may not unfairly be termed the foreign relations of Free Trade; and the benefits and blessings bound up with the cheap food of a people form just as surely the bright features of its domestic character.

At this important stage of Peter Leopold's policy—the general abolition throughout Tuscany of all restrictions on the trade in corn—the question very naturally presents itself, How came it that the beneficial effects of the free trade in cereals, introduced more than thirty years before into the Sienese Maremma, had not made themselves so felt and recognised that the extension of commercial liberty to the other Tuscan provinces was not earlier decreed? The true answer to this question must be given, not merely by the acts of Peter Leopold's own legislative and administrative attitude towards the Sienese Maremma, but by the previous ineffectual attempts to make and carry out laws for its welfare. We have seen that Pompeo Neri's plan for a Maremma Company was in reality a plan for the creation of a separate government, invested with powers as extensive as those of the East India Company, and aiming at a complete reformation of the whole political and social system. The views thus propounded by Neri and the Company, while based on the same he proposed to establish, were in truth the reflection of the arguments constantly held by one of the two classes of reformers, who, starting from quite different points of view, proposed to ameliorate the pestilential and poverty-stricken region. There were those who affirmed that great hydraulic operations should be effected to drain the marshes; that the

D

country would then become healthy, and that its population and cultivation would follow as a matter of course. Of these persons, the Jesuit Ximenes, a celebrated hydraulic engineer of those times, was the most important and influential. The draining of the Sienese Maremma was entrusted to him, and everything was expected from the result of his labours. His labours, however—the statement is made on the authority of Peter Leopold himself, towards the close of his reign—produced very insignificant and partial results, at an immense cost. Another class of reformers, whose views were directly or indirectly derived from the economic discourse of Bandini, held that the mere draining was only one, and that by no means the most important, element in the problem. The arguments advanced on this point by Bertolini, a high functionary connected with the Sienese Maremma, by Ortis, a most enlightened Venetian economist, who wrote much on the subject, and by Neri himself, possess beyond all question a revived interest at the present moment, when, through the plans of General Garibaldi, so many questions of the same character form the subject of public discussion in reference to the Roman Campagna. Bertolini, Ortis, and Neri all agreed that the great work, to be effectually carried out, must be done by raising the political and social level of the whole people. The attempts to form agricultural colonies, by dotting the Maremma here and there with little settlements of peasants from Lorraine, had signally failed. According to Neri and his friends, the work of improvement should rather be carried out concentrically from the points where, under whatever disadvantages, population already existed, and these points one should first attempt to improve. But the special improvement of the Maremma district must be chiefly influenced by the general improvement of the whole State. According as there should spring up a surplus population in the districts nearest the Maremma, that population would overflow into the Maremma itself, and this general increase of population in the State would chiefly be promoted by laws conferring on all classes the amplest liberty, extending that liberty to every part of the country, and so identifying it with its character and institutions, that the temptation would be held out to all in less favoured parts of the Peninsula to migrate into the Tuscan territory. " What," asked Ortis, " converted the wretched marshes and lagoons of Venice into a mighty State ? what renders the bleakest and most barren slopes of the Alps prized by the Swiss, for whom no other country possesses such attractions ? what has made the low unhealthy swamps of Holland the seat of a great and flourishing community ? One cause alone—that the ancient Venetian, the modern Swiss and Dutch, found there an amount of freedom of person and security of property which they would have vainly sought elsewhere. It is otherwise in the Sienese Maremma. The art of growing corn must be preceded and accompanied by the highest and noblest art of statesmanship—that of growing intelligent and active citizens." Nor, as will be afterwards seen, did the despotic prince of the house of Hapsburgh-Lorraine, who received such counsels, shrink from the legitimate and logical consequences of these premises. At the moment of bidding farewell to his Tuscan States, the prince, who at the commencement of his reign was chiefly engaged in the abolition of injurious corn-laws, was meditating at its close the best mode of conferring on his people a well-ordered system of representative government.

But the Free-Trade campaign of Tuscany now took another and scarcely less important form. It was not enough that Tuscans should possess the full liberty of buying and selling food, whether at home or from abroad. The artisan, the tradesman, the shopkeeper, the wholesale and retail merchant, master and apprentice alike, of whatever craft, must likewise possess the liberty of employing their skill and talent, of exchanging their capital or labour, of exercising their different trades, unfettered by any more binding and restrictive law than the great economic principle of demand and supply. To effect this change another revolution was required. The entire system of Florentine trade and manufactures had in the course of the Middle Ages been built up in a series of guilds. These manufacturing guilds and corporations had their own usages, their own law-courts, their own laws—laws as fixed and immutable as those of the Medes and the Persians. Though Neri did not share the opinions of the Tuscan economists and financiers of the old school, who believed that the prosperity of the country might be secured by a possible return to the manufacturing and commercial greatness of bygone days, though he was firmly convinced that Tuscany should concentrate her energies chiefly on the development of her agriculture, he was not the less persuaded that, low as Tuscan manufactures had sunk, they might again spring up—not certainly to their previous height, but to a much greater elevation—if only freed from the strong and close network of corporation rules and laws in which they were all fastened down. At his suggestion, and that of his colleague and fellow-reformer Tavanti, a commission was appointed to examine into the mode by which the national trade and manufactures might be restored to a healthier state. The commission soon reported that, though the government might not at once be able to do much good, it could prepare the way for future good by removing an immense amount of evil. Before, however, it could be practicable to restore manufactures and trade to a tolerable state, the great enemy must in some way or other be disposed of. And the great enemy standing in the way of all commercial and financial reform was the Appalto delle Finanze, or State Taxation Company. It had its contracts and its sub-contracts with all the ramifications of trade and commerce, and it was up in arms on the first suspicion that its interests could be in danger. The terms of the original concession had left to the sovereign the power, to be exercised under certain conditions, of revoking the Company's charter.   Peter Leopold did so by a decree of 26th August, 1767, granting to the Company full compensation for the profits which it might fairly reckon on during the four following years, as the charter did not expire until 1771.   Then, having cleared away the ground, and henceforth able to regard all financial questions from a single point of view, from one only looking at the direct interests of the State, Peter Leopold and his ministers began their great work of giving freedom to manufacturing labour, as they had already rendered free the trade in the produce of the soil.   By the law of 1st February, 1770, the different courts of the " merchants of wool," of silk, of physicians and apothecaries, of trunk-makers and tanners, of cloth-manufacturers and dealers, were, with all the special rights and privileges, and all the exclusive jurisdiction attached to the same, formally abolished.   In their place was created a " Chamber of Commerce, Art, and Manu-factures."   This last institution must not, however, be confounded with the Chamber of Commerce created at a later date in Tuscany, or the existing Chambers of Commerce now in full action all over Italy.   Peter Leopold's Chamber of Commerce proved to be, and in all likelihood was only intended to be, one of those temporary institutions by which, in the work of emanci-pating manufacturing labour, the sovereign here, as in other phases of his policy, sought gradually to accustom the public mind to the change from the old to the new state of things.   To an officer of this body there was, therefore, entrusted the right of hearing and deciding many cases which would previously have fallen under the jurisdiction of the tribunals just abolished.   But his award was not final.   An appeal lay from him to the regular law-courts.   In a short time, however, these merely transitional arrangements were done away with, and manufacturing industry was left completely free.

The change encountered the most violent opposition. Not merely all the class interests, but all the oldest and most inveterate class traditions and prejudices were ranged in favour of the old system.   Through its operation, it was declared the great cloth and silk manufactories of the Florentine Republic had grown up and flourished.   Every possible evil was predicted as likely to arise from the rashness of men who evinced so little respect "for the wisdom of their ancestors."   Municipal jealousy, equally with class prejudices, was opposed to the reform.   The entire organisation and working of all the legal and administrative powers of the Florence trade courts pre-supposed that the manufactures and trades of Florence should flourish at the expense of the other Tuscans in the provinces.   Just as in the higher departments of administration, the interests of Sienese, Pisan, or Pistojese citizens seemed only to exist for the purpose of giving places and profit to Florentine citizens, so even the common working of a wholesale or a retail business in Siena, in Pisa, or Pistoia was always subordinated to the supposed interests of rival tradesmen in the Tuscan capital.   Not only were countless difficulties thrown in the way of the manufacturers or workmen who from other parts of Tuscany might wish to settle in the capital, but peculiar privileges in the purchase of raw materials all over the country gave the Florentine a most unjust and unfair advantage over the other Tuscan producers.   The reforming prince and his ministers sought to combat popular prejudice by well-timed and ingenious appeals to popular sense and reason.   Sarchiani, the intimate friend of Tavanti the Finance Minister, wrote a charming little story, entitled, " Chinki: a Story of Cochin China, which may even furnish instruction for other places."   The witty writer, who, amongst the subjects of Peter Leopold, was the Tuscan forerunner of Harriet Martineau, reproduced in the hopeless confusion and complications of his Cochin China masters and workmen, wholesale

and retail dealers, the precise state of matters which at
the moment was engaging the attention of the Tuscan
lawgiver, and forming the theme of angry debates in
every workshop of Florence.   In kindred works of
popular fiction, the economic reformers of Tuscany, one
may here observe, had appealed likewise to the rural
classes, and had sought to enlist on their side the convictions of the country curate, the country surgeon,
the country lawyer, and that large and influential class—
the connecting link between the owners and cultivators
of the soil—the class of the land-stewards.   Although
not exactly in the strict chronological order of the
Leopoldine measures, it will perhaps be more in harmony with the chief spirit and aim of the present essay
to treat here of the next great—indeed, one may well
call it gigantic—step in his Free-Trade path.   He had
given, we have just seen, complete freedom of trade to
labour.   He had, we saw before, decreed freedom of
trade for the products of the soil.   He proceeded to do
something more—to establish freedom of trade in the
soil itself.   His law for the complete, or at least
nearly complete, abolition of entails gave to every
acre of ground within his dominions a character of
exchangeability and divisibility ; and if, as an eminent
contemporary economist not long ago reminded the
English public, exchangeability is not only the oldest,
but remains still the best synonym of economical
value, the importance of this prodigious economic
revolution can scarcely be over-stated.*   A short
account has already been given of the law restricting
entails promulgated by the regency on the 22nd of
June, 1747.   But the three classes of restrictions—relating to aristocratic qualification, to the duration and
to the object of entails—were much too slow in their
operations to produce the result desired by Peter

* I have said "nearly complete," because some imperial and other old fiefs
were left standing, and the complete abolition only dated from the introduction into Italy of the Code Napoléon.

Leopold and his statesmen. At the same time, the forty-two years between the first and final reform constituted a period quite long enough to make the public mind thoroughly familiar with the objects and benefits of the change ; and this very process of familiarising the public mind was, in the whole course of his reforming policy, one which Peter Leopold ever kept steadily in view. The final measure for the abolition of entails in Tuscany received the sanction of the sovereign on the 23rd of February, 1789 ; and it is instructive to observe that this crowning enactment, by which a state of things supposed to be eminently favourable to feudal and aristocratic privileges was swept away, became, as the logical result of forty years' previous legislation, the law of the land in this little Italian duchy ten weeks before the States-General of France opened the series of European revolutions at Versailles. But it was not by this law alone that through the Leopoldine legislation immense tracts of land, hitherto inalienable, were rendered the objects of contract and of sale. An account has already been given of the laws passed by the regency impeding the further accumulation of property, already so enormous, in the hands of the Church. But that arrangement possessed of itself a mere stationary character. Peter Leopold went further, and without having recourse to those sweeping measures of confiscation in which the later annals of Italy abound, he legalised certain pro- cesses of transfer by which the actual property of the Church lands passed into the hands of laymen on the payment of a small annual rent. The new lay pro- prietors could well afford to meet this charge, for the great agricultural improvement which the land received at their hands speedily created a margin of profit amply covering the annual payment which they had to make. By this arrangement the whole landed property of the country, whether held by the laity or the Church, became in one form or another a regular

and recognised element of commercial transactions. The
surplus capital realised in commerce could be invested
to any extent in landed property. The active and in-
dustrious tradesman, renewing the habits of his old
Florentine forefathers, could purchase from the decayed
noble a pleasant suburban villa ; and everywhere, as the
happy result of this change, the waste neglected lands
around the convent or the feudal castle became trans-
formed into well-ordered fields or smiling gardens. The
Tuscan nobles themselves were the first and greatest
gainers by this change. There is scarcely any fact more
clearly ascertained respecting the domestic economy of
the Florentine aristocracy during the period of the regency and at the accession of Peter Leopold than the uni-
versal inability to pay in money the wages of their
servants. They could only give them the corresponding
value in wine, oil, corn, &c. Towards the close of
Peter Leopold's reign, not only had this state of matters
ceased to exist, but many of the Florentine nobles were
able to make large advances to the manufacturing and
trading classes out of their accumulated savings. This
general freedom of internal trade was favoured and
fostered by an expansion of foreign trade, secured by the
application to the same of those identical principles of
commercial liberty so variously realised. In the year
after his accession, Peter Leopold had commanded preparations to be made for a general reform of the custom
system, and for the establishment of a new commercial
tariff. An entire period of fifteen years, from 1766 to
1781, elapsed before the final realisation of his orders.
The delay arose chiefly from his constant desire to proceed gradually and cautiously, and in great part from
the obstacles thrown in the way, first by the *Appalto
delle Finanze*, or State Taxation Company, and afterwards by the other enemies of improvement. Still,
every opportunity was seized to approach nearer and
nearer the wished-for goal. Much, we have already seen,
was done in connection with the abolition of the corn-

laws for the removal of the provincial customs barriers. Finally the law of 31st August, 1781, removed, with four exceptions, all the internal customs barriers, defined one uniform customs boundary—that of the State itself—and promulgated a very moderate general tariff for the introduction of all foreign produce into the country.* There were loud and angry cries from all the Tuscan producers, who descried in the effects of foreign competition a death-blow to native industry against the operation of the moderate Leopold tariff of 1781. The records of the Tuscan export trade have not justified their Protectionist jeremiad. We have seen how, judging from the data furnished to Count Carli by Gianni seven years before the accession of Peter Leopold, and whilst the old Protectionist system was everywhere in full force, the exports of Tuscany in that year (1757) amounted to 1,268,000 Tuscan crowns. Sixty years after the promulgation by Peter Leopold of his moderate customs tariff, in 1841, the same export trade amounted to 5,428,571 Tuscan crowns. And even this scarcely gives a fair result, for, as we shall have occasion to observe, the operation of the moderate Leopoldine tariff during these sixty years was too often interrupted, and reaction at home, and revolutionary foreign influences from abroad, combined to interfere with its normal action.

There is one great difficulty in doing full justice to the commercial policy of Peter Leopold and his wise minister Pompeo Neri when we attempt to treat that policy as a single and separate theme. Thus treated, the examination remains extremely imperfect, because it formed, in truth, but one branch of a noble, stately, deep-rooted tree, of which the other branches bear the names of ecclesiastical reform, criminal legislation, local government and taxation, and in foreign policy peace and non-intervention. On the vast subject of the eccle-

---

* The general character of the Tuscan tariff, as modified by the law of Peter Leopold's son and successor, Ferdinand III., will be discussed in detail further on.

siastical reforms—one so vast and so comprehensive that the words "Leopoldine legislation" are not unfrequently used by Italian writers to denote that alone—it would, for many and obvious reasons, be quite out of place to enter here. It has been incidentally referred to solely in connection with those changes in the holding of Church property by which greater free-dom was given to the sale and transfer of land.* It will in future be referred to only in so far as the opposition which Peter Leopold's Church reforms provoked, took sometimes the form of an agitation against his com-mercial policy. The system of local government intro-duced throughout the duchy, though for various reasons less liberal than that previously given by Pompeo Neri to the communes of the Milan duchy, can be referred to here only in connection with the powers of local government and taxation acquired by the communes, and which, of course, they had infinite modes of exercising for the furtherance or the injury of both agriculture and commerce. Their action in the matter of *octroi* duties was limited to Florence, Siena, Pistoia, and Pisa—the four towns which, probably under the pres-sure of strong local influences, Peter Leopold had excepted from the general abolition of the internal custom-houses. Of his mild criminal legislation I will only venture to remark, that perhaps too exclu-sive a merit has been ascribed to it in estimating that general mildness of Tuscan manners which ought certainly to be traced in part to the absence of many forms of temptations to crime, forms which must be considered the natural results of misery and want. But there is one feature of the Leopoldine policy of which, however, the merit must be shared by Peter Leopold with his father the Emperor Grand-Duke Francis, which

---

* It might, in relation to the transfer and sale of land, have received a much greater extension, had it been viewed in its connection with the sup-pression of the Order of the Jesuits and the vast amount of landed property which that event placed at the disposal of the State.

cannot receive too great prominence in the present essay. I refer to the mode in which the father proclaimed and the son renewed the proclamation, that the observance of a complete neutrality in the contests of other States was a fundamental principle of their rule. This enlightened foreign policy at once brought with it its own reward. The declaration that the Tuscan State renounced its traditional attitude of hostility to the Mahometan powers at once revived its trade with the Levant, and permanently settled what might be termed its Eastern question, in a profitable and pacific sense. Nor is the lesson which this little State gave a hundred years ago unworthy even now of the thoughtful meditation of much greater powers. Yet one thing more was wanting to complete the majestic edifice of the Leopoldine policy. That one thing was the granting, as he had firmly intended, and as indeed his whole system of local government seemed to foreshadow, representative institutions to his people. How and why that purpose was thwarted it were vain here to inquire. The last year of his rule over Tuscany was passed amidst the first rolling thunders of the French Revolution. And when, on the death of his brother Joseph, he handed over the rule of Tuscany to a regency, and, bidding an affectionate farewell to his people, repaired to Vienna, he found himself the central point and representative of dynastic fears and hatreds widely different from the noble reforming aims and acts with which his name and fame in the world's history will be indissolubly linked.

IV.

ALL the forms of human progress are allied and inter-dependent. Whoever seeks to promote any one will speedily find himself, by an inexorable law, attracted to, and engaged in the furtherance of, another. The sovereigns of the house of Hapsburgh-Lorraine began their career of civil and economic reforms by two very simple acts—one, compelling the clergy as well as the laity to pay taxes ; the other, allowing the free export and import of corn in the Sienese Maremma.

It does not fall within the province of this essay to follow out the many and important consequences of the first of the two acts ; but, as regards the second, it is instructive to observe that, before long, the sovereign and statesmen of Tuscany had the conclusion forced upon them that, to secure agricultural and commercial progress in this very Sienese Maremma, it was neces-sary that many other things should be done besides the removal of protective and prohibitory duties; that citizens must have equal rights ; that public health must be secured ; that public morality must be raised ; in a word, that the entire standard of society must be elevated to a much higher level. Having formed this conclusion respecting the Sienese Maremma, they soon found it necessary to act on the same principle in the entire Tuscan State ; or, rather, they found that the first attempts must remain mutilated and incomplete, unless supplemented by the second. The contemporary observers and chroniclers of this great work of ameliora-tion—as we have seen in the writings of the Venetian Ortis—pushed these conclusions to political, as well as civil and social consequences, and dwelt on the necessity

—one which Peter Leopold and his advisers themselves recognised—of giving stability to these reforms, by creating a system of popular representation.

And if it be true that all the forms of progress and improvement hang together, it is not the less certain that an equally close connection exists between all the varieties of abuse, of wrong-doing, and corruption. No sooner had the reformer quitted his States than the reaction sprang up in every corner of them. He thought that he had cast out for ever the evil spirit of Protectionism. It was soon seen returning to its ancient haunts; and when we say that in its company appeared popular ignorance, religious fanaticism, mob fury, the jealousy and suspicion of the good, the intrigues and calumnies of the bad, base ingratitude towards benefactors, and a systematic hostility to progress—when we say that in its company appeared these grim and ghastly images, it is surely no mere figure of speech to affirm that it brought back with it seven other spirits more wicked than itself.

An agitation, strongly though secretly favoured by all who believed that they had lost in personal influence or interests by the Leopoldine reforms, broke out into popular tumults, first in Pistoia, then in Leghorn, finally in Florence. In the two first towns the demands of the rioters were confined to the revocation of the Leopoldine measures for the reform of the Church. At Florence they combined with the same the further demand that the Leopoldine laws authorising Free Trade in corn and the free manufacture and sale of bread should be repealed, and that there should be again called into existence the ancient organisation of the Grascieri, or corn and bread inspectors, without whose permission, in the good old times, not a sack of corn could be bought, or a loaf of bread baked or sold.

It appears but too certain that, with one illustrious exception, the members of the council of regency, appointed on his departure by Peter Leopold, were

amongst the chief instigators of the troubles. The illustrious exception was Francesco Gianni, the last survivor
of that noble triumvirate of economic reformers—
Pompeo Neri and Angelo Tavanti being the two others
—who in this branch of statesmanship have imparted
so bright a lustre to Peter Leopold's reign. The only
name worthy to be placed beside theirs is that of their
renowned colleague, Giulio Rucellai, but his sphere of
action was almost entirely confined to ecclesiastical
policy. Peter Leopold had, doubtless, believed that the
participation of Gianni in the regency would be a
guarantee for the preservation of his great measures of
commercial freedom ; but it was precisely the prominent
part taken by him in the same, and the influence and
honour thereby procured, which rendered him an object
of bitter jealousy and hatred to his colleagues. Accord-
ingly, he was represented to the rioters as the cause of
the then high price of food, 1790 happening to be
rather a dear year. His house was attacked and sacked,
and he only found safety by instant flight to Bologna,
where a communication from his colleagues of the
regency soon followed him, to the effect that the state
of popular exasperation against him in Florence rendered
most unadvisable his return. In nearly all these popular
troubles the mob sought a relief for its supposed suffer-
ings and wrongs in one old and infallible specific—that
of mulcting or massacring Jews. At Leghorn a heavy
contribution was levied on the Jews' quarter. At
Florence matters went further, and it was resolved to
sack the Ghetto, and make short work of its inhabitants.
If the resolution was frustrated, the result was mainly
due to the truly Christian fortitude of the then Arch-
bishop of Florence, Martini, who, on hearing of the
imminent danger, rushed out from his own palace,
situate close to the Jews' quarter, placed himself at the
entrance of the Ghetto, and declared that the rioters
should only enter by passing over his body. More
fortunate than later prelates, whose lot has been cast in

times of equal trouble, the heroic bearing of their chief pastor daunted and cowed the Florence rioters, and they fell back in shame and silence from the objects of their intended prey. The Jews of Siena not long afterwards, in one of these mob outbreaks, were not so fortunate.   In that city the partisans of 1789 had planted in the great square a tree of liberty. It was cut down and set fire to by the lovers of the good old times, who, to make the demonstration still more effective, seized and bound five Jews, threw them into the flames, and then and there roasted them alive. The published justification of the deed exculpated, however, the Sienese Jews from any special attachment to the principles of the Gallic revolution of '89, and described the act as having a mere precautionary and monitory character, inspired by the conviction that the mere sight of a pole erected in a public square *must* call forth amongst Sienese Israelites the instinctive passion and inherent habit of crucifying little Christian children.

When the news reached Peter Leopold at Vienna that in the said week of May his old Tuscan capital had been the scene of such troubles, and that in consequence the regency, on the 8th of June, had issued an edict suspending provisionally all Free Trade in corn, he gave vent to the very natural indignation felt at this summary undoing of the good work achieved during his reign. But it is not easy to divine why so long a period as six months should have elapsed before the appearance of the edict of the 27th of December, in which he decreed that the Free Trade in cereals should be replaced on its former footing. One may, perhaps, be allowed to conjecture that he wished the legislative re-enactment to be accompanied by the very remarkable appeal to his people which at the same time was published. The riots in Tuscany had too clearly shown how ignorant large masses of the people were respecting the true spirit of his policy, and what selfish interests were at work to keep them in that ignorance. Peter Leopold accordingly commanded the publication of "The Government of Tuscany," a work of which the chief share in the composition has been commonly ascribed to the constant and enlightened friend of Free Trade, that very Francesco Gianni, against whom the intrigues of his colleagues and the passions of the Florence mob had been so signally directed. In the memorable account of his stewardship, thus spontaneously given by the reforming prince, we are told in the introduction that it was called forth by the conviction that honest governments have nothing to lose, but everything to gain, when the strongest light is thrown on all their acts ; and that the throwing of such light is precisely the best security against the arts of the ill-disposed and the evil-doer. The work passes successively in review the civil, criminal, ecclesiastical, and financial state of Tuscany. One fact taken from its criminal statistics speaks of itself volumes. We are told that in the year 1788, during a period of twenty-two days, no person in any part of the State had been committed to prison, simply because during that period in the whole State—and it numbered above a million souls—not a single new crime had been committed. The volume was chiefly instructive from the light thrown by it on the interdependence of all the various kinds of administrative reform. We see the connection in the legislator's mind between his agricultural ameliorations, his abolition of all exclusive class privileges and monopolies, his entail laws, his restoration to general commerce of the Church lands, his encouragement of academies for science and the fine arts, his efforts to raise the standard of female education, and his somewhat amusing and patriarchal crusade against expensive fashions in dress and luxuries in general. One fact may be stated, more amusing than important, just because it shows that the most consistent and virtuous of Free Traders is not, any more than other frail mortals,

E

exempt from the weaknesses of humanity. This great reformer—who reversed the entire system of the country's taxation, to secure freedom of contract and of sale to capital and labour; who braved the hostility alike of nobles and Churchmen that he might throw into the market, if circumstances required it, every landed estate within the Tuscan boundaries; who proclaimed so moderate a commercial tariff; who has a right to be considered, if any sovereign ever had that right, the royal representative of Free Trade in all its forms— actually set afoot and headed, at the close of his reign, a little Protectionist revolt against his own régime, and— Free Trader on all other points—might have excited the envy of Colbert himself in his zeal for the protection of native Tuscan wool!

In the special part of the work relating to the financial progress of the country are given the following details:—" At the accession of Peter Leopold the public debt amounted to 87,559,775 Tuscan lire.* Savings had been effected under various forms, which were calculated at 12,083,629 Tuscan lire, from which, however, 3,762,816 must be deducted, as that sum had to be sent to Vienna. The public revenue was estimated at 8,058,685 Tuscan lire, and as the population numbered 945,863 souls, the taxes came to just nine Tuscan lire a head. The ordinary expenditure was 7,685,152 Tuscan lire, and the extraordinary expenditure 763,739 Tuscan lire, thus leaving an annual surplus of 509,793 Tuscan lire." When Peter Leopold published the accounts of his government during a period of twenty-four years, to the end of 1789, the public revenue amounted to 9,199,121 Tuscan lire, and the population had increased to 1,058,000 souls, each Tuscan thus paying about eight and a half Tuscan lire a head. The increase of income and diminution of public burdens furnished the most luminous proof of the progress of the country. It must be remembered, moreover, that every year great works of agricultural

* A Tuscan lira was 84 centimes.

improvement, drainage, &c., were effected by the annual savings, which, during the entire period of Peter Leopold's reign, amounted to 38,762,854 Tuscan lire. It was thus in his power to execute great public works without contracting loans, or imposing new burdens to any sensible extent on his subjects.

Peter Leopold had formally promised that the independence of Tuscany, as a separate State, should be established by the complete transfer of the sovereignty to his second son, Ferdinand. This took place on the 22nd of February, 1791. In the year that elapsed until Peter Leopold's death, which occurred on the 29th of February, 1792, the Tuscan State already began to feel the effects of the general change, as regarded reform and progress, in the attitude of the House of Hapsburgh-Lorraine. It appears certain that the desire of the now Emperor Leopold to conciliate the religious feelings of his Flemish subjects re-acted on the policy of his son, the Grand Duke of Tuscany, for not a few of the religious corporations abolished by Peter Leopold were re-established in the commencement of the Grand Duke Ferdinand's reign, involving, of course, the partial restoration to those bodies of the landed property which they had possessed. It was equally evident that the system of commercial freedom sanctioned by the father was about to receive fresh wounds under the government of the son. The most permanent effect of this Protectionist tendency was the change, not indeed very great, but in an undoubted Protectionist sense, in the general customs tariff of 1781. But other effects were too clearly visible. The harvest of 1792 had been a scanty one. Leghorn became the scene of another popular agitation against the export of corn. This led to the publication, on the 9th of October, of a government decree prohibiting the exportation from the grand duchy of corn, hay, vegetables, chestnuts, flour of whatever quality, &c. This, the second Protectionist outbreak in Tuscany after Peter Leopold's departure from the State, was hailed everywhere

by the ignorant and prejudiced mob with undisguised
delight.   The re-action made rapid progress.   Although
this edict of the 9th of October had declared that the
free circulation of corn, &c., in the interior of the grand
duchy should remain unchanged, it was quickly followed
by another decree, on the 30th of the same month,
creating a new body of controllers of public food, termed
" Presidenti delle Vettovaglie."   These presidents of the
" victuals " were in reality invested with the powers of
the former Grascieri and officers of abundance, suppressed
by Peter Leopold, and with precisely the same result;
for, as the officers of abundance had everywhere guaran-
teed scarcity, the presidents of the victuals soon found
themselves in a fair way of having no victuals to preside
over.   One of their first measures was to prohibit the
free circulation of corn throughout the grand duchy, and
one of the first consequences of this measure was the
following.   Not the least remarkable effect of Peter
Leopold's Free-Trade legislation in the matter of cereals
had been its tendency to promote agricultural progress
and traffic, not only in his own States, but on all the
land bordering on the same in the Papal provinces of
the Romagna and the Marches.   Notwithstanding all
the obstacles thrown by the Papal legislation in the way
of exporting corn, it was reckoned that not less than
three million sacks of corn found their way annually
from the Papal frontier to Leghorn, and that, by the
mere transit of the same, Tuscany made a profit on each
sack of three Tuscan lire.   These nine millions of Tuscan
lire ceased, of course, through the prohibition of the
government, and the restrictive action of the presidents
of the victuals, to flow into Tuscany.   This was only
one of the more prominent forms of the mischief which
made itself, before long, so keenly and so generally felt,
that on the 17th of August, 1795, another grand ducal
edict appeared, restoring the internal corn trade to its
previous freedom, and suppressing the office of the
presidents of the victuals.   In the proclamation accom-

panying the edict, the Grand Duke Ferdinand frankly confessed that in the temporary return to a Protectionist system he had committed an immense mistake, and that a vast amount of public money had been hopelessly squandered in the attempt to furnish his subjects, by means of government arrangements and control, with those food supplies which could only be regularly and securely obtained by the action of Free Trade. In making this avowal, the grand duke gave expression to the opinions of the most enlightened and important amongst the various Tuscan municipalities. He had made a direct appeal to these bodies by a government circular of the 7th of August, 1794, requesting them to declare fully and frankly their experience and convictions on the results of his father's Free-Trade legislation. The answers varied, of course, according to the various degrees of intelligence and public spirit in the different munici- palities, but the preponderating mass of testimony was in favour of the great benefits accruing from Peter Leopold's Free-Trade legislation. The partisans of com- mercial liberty did everything in their power to aid at this period, by means of the press, the grand duke's return to the liberal policy of his father. There appeared at this time several popular works of great ability, illus- trating the beneficent results of the Leopoldine laws, and instituting detailed comparisons between the progress of Tuscany under the Free-Trade régime, and the con- dition of the European States in which Protectionist systems were in full force. But the economic history of Tuscany was now doomed to reflect the (for it) most calamitous phases of the French revolutionary annals. All the States of Europe found themselves drawn within the orbit of the great political movement which had its seat and centre in Paris. The two first sovereigns of the House of Hapsburgh-Lorraine had, as was already stated, done everything in their power to secure for their little State the benefits of a perpetual neutrality. The Emperor Grand Duke Francis had formally proclaimed the neutrality o the grand duchy at the close of 1739. In 1771 Pompeo Neri, by the command of Peter Leopold, studied the question of neutrality in all its details, and drew up what might be termed a charter of neutrality, in which its proclamation and maintenance were declared to be fundamental laws of the State. Neri, in the series of reasonings by which his plan was accompanied, set forth the financial and commercial grounds, the logical harmony of this principle of perpetual neutrality with the policy of Free Trade established in the State. Seven years later, Peter Leopold issued, on the 1st of August, 1778, the law in which he declared that neutrality was a constitutional, fundamental, and perpetual principle of the grand duchy. Now, even amidst the general European agitations consequent on the movement of republican France, Peter Leopold's son Ferdinand sought honestly to adhere to the principles of neutrality professed by his father and his grandfather. The resident agent of the French Republic at the court of Florence informed his government that the Tuscan ruler and his ministers were both strenuous and sincere in their attempts to preserve neutrality, but that the anti-Gallican feeling of the population was generally too strong to allow the government to give effect to its friendly purposes. Indeed, the position of the Grand Duke Ferdinand was by no means enviable ; for, whilst making every effort to maintain the neutrality of his little State, he had to endure the reproaches of the other Italian princes for his lukewarmness to the cause of Royalty, and the taunts of his own subjects, who accused him of a culpable indifference to the fate of his aunt, Marie Antoinette. The combined pressure put upon him by his own brother, the Emperor Francis, by the other Italian princes, and by his anti-Gallican subjects, had at last the effect of involving the Grand Duke Ferdinand in the war between Austria and France ; and on the morning of the 25th of March, 1799, Florence was occupied by French troops. Tuscan neutrality disappeared in the presence of a *force majeure*. But it was something to have upheld it for sixty years, under trials and temptations of no common order, to have exempted Tuscan property and life from the calamitous results entailed on the States which had taken part in the conflicts of Frederick the Great and Maria Theresa, or which had during the previous nine years been so terribly associated with the rise of the French Republic. It was something to have stood forth alone amongst civilised States as the representative of principles so wise and so beneficent in themselves, and to have bequeathed those principles to the Italy of after times. Nor should it be forgotten that in the first adoption and proclamation of this principle of neutrality, and in its subsequent elevation, by Peter Leopold, to the character of a fundamental law of the State, Tuscany began by abjuring a long-established tradition of its foreign policy. It abandoned the system in force during two centuries of chronic hostility to the Moslem powers. It reconsidered its "Eastern question" from a more rational, a more international, and a much more profitable point of view, and sixty years of peaceful trading with the Levant was its appropriate recompense.

The first French occupation of Tuscany, commencing in March, 1799, and closing in the July of the same year, throws little light on the history of Free Trade, though it throws a very strong light on all points connected with the free appropriation of the pictures and statues in the possession of invaded States. This is not the place to dwell on the romantic wanderings of the Venus de Medici, during her attempt to escape from her Gallic wooers, on her hurried flight southwards to the congenial shores of Sicily, or on the means by which she was thence removed, not so much *vi et armis*, as by being treacherously decoyed, and entrapped, and borne away from those shores to her new shrine at the Louvre. The nature of this narrative compels me to turn away from so fascinating a theme, and to record the economic

triumphs of the Florentine Senate, which, after having
lain dormant for a period of 264 years, suddenly awoke
from its long slumber in the July of 1799, and finding
itself, by the accidents of a revolutionary period, in the possession of supreme power, shortly proceeded to organise,
or rather disorganise, the commercial system of the
country after its own peculiar fashion.   By its decrees
of the 25th of July and 23rd of September, it undertook
the task of establishing the price of corn, of flour, and of
bread.   More speedily and effectually to secure these
results, it decreed that all owners of corn should declare
the amount in their possession, and that six " normal
ovens " should be opened in Florence, where bread
should be sold at the prices fixed by the far-seeing
Senate.   But the owners of corn, under the apprehension
that they must pay taxes in proportion to the quantity
declared, sent in declarations far short of the real
amount ; and the alarm caused by a not over-plentiful
harvest was increased tenfold by the reports of its
being even scantier than was actually the case.   The
natural consequence of the operation of the Senate's
normal ovens was that of ruining most of the private
bakers ; and, in the hopeless confusion and embarrass-
ment thus brought about, bread rose to a monstrous
price.   The Florentine Senate did not confine its labours
to mere economic matters.   Deploring, apparently, the
culpable leniency by which, eleven years before, no
criminal, during a period of twenty-two days, had been
consigned to a Tuscan prison, the Florentine Senate in-
stituted, during its eleven months' rule, twenty-two
thousand criminal prosecutions.   Every prison in the
State was full to overflowing, and the enormous majority
of the prisoners were charged with political offences.
The Florentine Senate had invented a new term in the
criminal law of Tuscany to designate the offence which it
had in most abhorrence, and mere suspicion of " genialità
Francese," or a supposed inclination to the principles of
the French Revolution, was held to be sufficient justifi-

cation for tearing inoffensive citizens from their families and homes, and consigning them to the dungeons of Volterra, or to the fellowship of the galley-slaves of Leghorn. The hatred generated by these acts did not give way to gratitude for the paternal care with which the Florentine Senate—that its policy respecting wine might be on a level with that respecting bread—decreed that throughout Tuscany wine should henceforth be sold only by the wine-growers themselves, or by licensed innkeepers. At last the echoes of the general complaint reached the Grand Duke Ferdinand, at Vienna, and His Imperial and Royal Highness, by an edict of the 19th of June, 1800, thanked the Florentine Senate for the great ability and zeal displayed by it in the temporary government of the State during such troublesome times ; adding, however, that he had no further use for its services. A commission of regency was appointed in its place. But the battle of Marengo suddenly changed the entire political aspect of Italy ; and in the October of 1800, the French troops, under Generals Dupont and Miolis, again occupied Tuscany. It appeared, however, at that moment, to Bonaparte more important to con-ciliate the Spanish Bourbons by ceding to a Bourbon prince the little State of the Grand Duke Ferdinand, than to annex the grand duchy to France. And, accord-ingly, by one of the provisions of the treaty of Luneville, Tuscany was transferred to the Infante Louis of Parma, who received the title of King of Etruria. The economic history of Tuscany during the short reign of King Louis, and, after his death, during the regency exercised by his widow in the name of her young son, may be almost wholly summed up in one little sentence. It was a succession of attempts to defraud the public creditors. The extravagance of the regent-mother knew no bounds, and her advisers could imagine no better means of meeting financial difficulties than by arbitrarily reducing the five per cent. securities to three per cent. ; and, finally, by paying no interest whatever. The remonstrances addressed to the regent-mother by one of Tuscany's greatest statesmen, Vittorio Fossombroni, arrested, but only for a very short period, the downward course of the State towards complete bankruptcy. And that stage would speedily have been reached, had not the arbiter of States and sovereigns at the Tuileries changed his intention with reference to the fate of Tuscany ; and, by the treaty of Fontainbleau, of the 27th of October, 1807, united that State to the French Empire, where it formed the three departments of the Mediterranean, the Arno, and the Ombrone.

It would be, at first sight, absurd for a single moment to suppose that, under the régime of the imperial author of the Berlin and Milan decrees, the economic system of Peter Leopold could during the next seven years present any other aspect than that of a suspended vitality. And yet this would be a view far from correct. The real truth was that the operation of the Code Napoleon, and generally of the Napoleonic legislation and administration, supplemented in many points the reform which Peter Leopold had commenced, but which his son, the Grand Duke Ferdinand, and the short-lived government of the Etrurian kingdom, had not carried out in a kindred spirit. I have already mentioned that part of the Church lands had, contrary to the provisions of the Leopoldine legislation, been withdrawn by his successor from the ordinary course and conditions of trade in landed property, and been restored to the clerical owners. Under the French Empire all this was reversed, and, though provisions were made in favour of certain charitable and educational orders, all religious corporations were abolished, and their property either diverted to purposes of public utility, or divided and put up for sale. To the Code Napoleon Tuscany likewise owed a measure greatly promoting the facility and security of all commercial dealings in land—I refer to the obligatory registration of all mortgages on property, and the power obtained by all interested to inspect the same.

It is impossible to over-rate the fresh impulse, and the greater security which these two acts imparted to the acquisition of landed property. The imperial decree completely suppressing the religious corporations bears date the 29th of April, 1808. In other respects the Napoleonic system pointed in the same direction. Thus the provision of the code by which, in the division of landed property, daughters shared equally with sons, had the natural tendency of breaking up still more the large estates. Then the greater simplicity and economy of judicial proceeding likewise bore their useful fruits. Every man in the country felt the benefit accruing from the better regulation of the public debt, and from that security of public credit which contrasted so favourably with the imminent bankruptcy of the short-lived Etrurian kingdom. And if large sums of money were taken from the Tuscan people in the form of taxes, every Tuscan could see with his own eyes that large sums of money were likewise expended in all directions on new or improved roads and bridges; that every market was thus brought nearer to the peasant farmer's grange; that his labour was lightened, and that his profits were increased. One may be permitted to doubt whether one prominent feature of the Napoleonic legislation was so much appreciated in Tuscany as in other countries— I refer to the complete abolition of noble rights and privileges, and the placing all citizens on a common level. The fact was that everything really valuable and effective in this direction had been done already, and that the most generous boons of any republican or imperial fiat were but feeble copies of the blessings bestowed many years before on his subjects by an Austrian archduke. At the same time due weight must be given to the fact that, by the Code Napoleon, the last imperial, republican, and Medicean fiefs left standing by Peter Leopold were all, without exception, swept away. The abolition of entails became complete. There could be little foreign commerce in Tuscany or elsewhere under the sharp watch of the English cruisers, yet there is good reason to believe that, from whatever reason, the Emperor Napoleon, in dealing with Leghorn, showed a disposition to wink at the evasion of his own iron-bound continental system. The inexorable logic of the Berlin and Milan decrees, and the Protective policy to which they bound down the whole imperial administration, made themselves felt all the same in 1812, in Tuscany, in their most characteristic forms. The imperial decree of that year, which fixed the maximum price of corn for the whole empire at 33 francs the hectolitre, found the price of cereals in Tuscany much above that figure. The prefect of the Arno contrived, in his application of the decree, to make a bad state of matters infinitely worse, so that the price of corn in the Florence market rose to 80 francs the hectolitre. This enormous price was due to the commercial confusion, rivalling that brought about by the doings of the Florentine Senate, some years before, and directly resulting from other edicts compelling the bakers to sell bread at a price quite impracticable in the then state of the flour market. These consequences of the economic legislation of the first French empire, shortly before its collapse, could only have had the effect of the more endearing to all rational and reflecting Tuscans that wise system of economic legislation from which their country had in past times derived such signal benefits.

When, at last, the first French Empire fell, and the Grand Duke Ferdinand assumed again the rule of the Tuscan State, it was the signal good fortune of Tuscany that he placed at the head of the administration Vittorio Fossombroni. In the annals of Tuscan reform, and more especially in those of sound economic policy, this truly great statesman holds a place second only to that of Pompeo Neri. The lives of those two men cover the entire period of time from 1706 to 1844. Their unbroken political action extends from 1727 to the last of these two dates, for Pompeo Neri had already distinguished himself in the service of the State at the age of twenty-one, and at the period of Neri's death, in 1776, Vittorio Fossombroni was twenty-two years of age, and had already distinguished himself by his rare abilities as a hydraulic engineer. Though Fossombroni's life was protracted until the age of ninety, he preserved his marvellous intellect clear and undisturbed until the very last, so that Tuscany, in the thirty years which elapsed from the fall of the first Napoleon until Fossombroni's death, had the fortune to be always guided by a statesman in whose mind there dwelt, with peculiar force and freshness, the economic traditions of that Leopoldine government under which he had himself played a conspicuous part, who had lived through and striven against the successive Protectionist re-actions which it was our duty to record, by whose wise counsels the spendthrift Queen Regent of Etruria had been arrested, though for too brief a period, in her course of reckless extravagance, and whose moral influence over Napoleon I., when the power of the great conqueror and lawgiver reached its height, was ever employed for the best interests of his Tuscan fellow-citizens. Fossombroni, like Neri, served the cause of commercial liberty by his pen, not less efficiently than by his counsels in the cabinet. It was after his withdrawal from all participation in the wretched misgovernment of the Queen Regent of Etruria that he employed his leisure in the composition of a work, "Ideas on Commercial Restraints," in which the whole question of commercial freedom is treated in that spirit of sincere conviction respecting its principles and practice which his experience as a Tuscan citizen had so strongly generated. If Pompeo Neri may justly be regarded as the statesman who did most to found the economic liberty in Tuscany, Vittorio Fossombroni has an equal right to be gratefully remembered as the minister who chiefly contributed to secure and consolidate the same. Commercial liberty, no more than any other form of freedom, was in favour with the imperial and royal members of the Holy Alliance, whose words, for so many years after the fall of the first Napoleon, gave law to all Italy; and it is probable that, but for the great personal influence of Fossombroni, and the well-deserved esteem in which he was held by all the courts and cabinets of Europe, the little State of Tuscany would not have been allowed to re-establish, after 1814, a system of commercial policy so directly at variance with the one in force in the other parts of the peninsula. But the counsels and remonstrances of the venerable minister, whose words had been listened to with equal reverence in the cabinet of Peter Leopold and his son, and in the senate of the first Napoleon, possessed, even amongst Metternichs and Nesselrodes, a moral authority far outweighing the political importance of the petty Italian duchy which Fossombroni represented. The admirers of Prince Talleyrand are in the habit of citing, as a proof of his enlightened, progressive, and philanthropic mind, the spirit in which he proposed that the little kingdom of Belgium should be founded and built up, and the plans which he set forth for so rendering that State a model government to all others in the nineteenth century, that its safety should rest less on the express stipulations of written treaties than on the general respect and gratitude of Europe. The reader of Fossombroni's "Ideas on Commercial Restraints" will have little difficulty in recognising the fact that kindred ideas and aspirations animated the writer; and the feeling of gratitude for his services, and veneration towards his memory, entertained by all classes of the Tuscan people, is certainly not lessened just at this moment by the recollection that the statesman who, during so long a period, as the minister of an absolute sovereign, wielded almost unchecked power over the State of Tuscany, was, amongst all politicians of the nineteenth century, the one who ever hoped least and spoke most slightingly of government superintendence and control; who hoped most from, and counted most on, the natural and free expansion of individual and social energies, and who, when often entreated by fussy and fidgetty theorists to undertake the direction of other people's business, would shrug his shoulders, and mildly answer, "Just let people look after their own business, they know it far better than any minister of state."

V.

PROTECTIONIST re-actions live long and die hard. The House of Hapsburgh-Lorraine ruled over Tuscany from 1737 till 1859. Free Trade was the avowed spirit of its commercial policy. During that period it was strongly distinguished from all other European States by the desire to give legislative effect to its principles; yet it cannot be said, even when its rule came to a close, that the practice had been constantly and consistently in accordance with the theory. On one point, however, there exists no doubt. During this period—from the restoration of 1814 to 1859—those Free-Trade principles which, under the regency governing for the Emperor Grand Duke Francis, and during all Peter Leopold's reign, had been at first only the possession of economists like Bandini, and of statesmen like Neri, Tavanti, and Gianni, and of the comparatively small group of en-lightened politicians who shared their views, became with each succeeding year more and more the economic creed of the whole Tuscan people. From 1737 until the close of the eighteenth century the government had been far ahead of the people. It is pretty certain that during the last twenty years of the period from 1814 to 1859 the position had become reversed, and the people—at least all the higher and educated classes—were ahead of the government.

Such, however, was not the state of matters imme-diately after the restoration. It was a misfortune for Tuscany—one of which the full effects were not per-ceived until a later period—that a good many months elapsed before the return to Tuscany of the restored Grand Duke Ferdinand and the formal appointment as his two chief ministers of Vittorio Fossombroni and Neri Corsini. Prince Rospigliosi, who provisionally administered the State, and his chief adviser, Frullani, were too much inclined to retrograde courses, and did not confront in the fitting spirit the new Protectionist reaction which very soon made itself felt. In its immediate influence on Free Trade the restored government did both good and evil. It abolished many foolish administrative regulations and police restrictions on the free exercise of trade which had sprung up during the French occupation; it swept away a number of *octroi* establishments which had cramped the free movement of internal commerce; and it restored the trade in grain and the manufacture and the sale of bread to the complete independence which they had obtained under the old Leopoldine laws. But its policy was not equally sound in other respects. Reversing the action of the Napoleonic government—which had suppressed the religious orders, and applied the greater portion of their landed property to the extinction of the national debt—it at once re-established these orders, and withdrew from the ordinary conditions of the trade in land property to the amount of four millions of Tuscan lire, which it restored to the former owners. In another respect it reversed the policy of the Napoleonic government, which had suppressed the last vestige of entails by depriving of all their feudal rights such imperial and Medicean fiefs as had still remained untouched by Peter Leopold's legislation; if these were not recalled into life, a new class of entails, for such they virtually were, was created by conferring on the Knights of the revived Order of St. Stephen the right of rendering inalienable in perpetuity properties of the value of ten thousand Tuscan crowns, which thus acquired for all practical purposes the precise character of the entails that had been swept away. I purposely use the word entails, though the *fidei commissary* arrangements, both in their previous and revived form,

F

do not in all respects exactly coincide with our notion of entail ; but both in principle and practice they have so much, not only in common, but quite identical, that I have thought it best to employ throughout the more familiar English word. Nor were these reactionary tendencies confined to internal laws and government. They were equally reflected in the mode observed on the re-establishment of the Tuscan customs tariff. The first general tariff of Peter Leopold—that issued in 1781 —had been remarkable for the extreme moderation of the duties imposed on the import of foreign manufactures, and on the export of native raw materials. In that first Protectionist reaction by which, as we have seen, the early years of the Grand Duke Ferdinand's reign were marked, the tariff of 1781 had received (in 1791) not a few important modifications, all of them more or less in a Protectionist sense. The restoration of 1814, instead of returning to the more liberal tariff of 1781, recalled into existence that framed ten years later. At the period of its revival, in 1814, its provisions still contrasted by their liberality with the tariffs of every other European State, but it was not the less a falling back from, not an advance beyond, the best period of the Leopoldine commercial legislation.

Fossombroni has been often taxed with want of sufficient firmness and energy, because the Tuscany which was confided to his administration, and of which for thirty years he had the supreme direction, did not at once, on regaining its position as an independent European State, reproduce in full and unbroken harmony the fairest characters of its early commercial progress. But no accusation can possibly be more unjust ; Fossombroni had to contend for every inch of ground in the Congress of Vienna, where he was striving to keep the independence of the Tuscan State free from an overshadowing Austrian supremacy, and to maintain in honour Tuscan traditions of Free Trade, when traditions or principles of freedom of any kind whatever were remorselessly proscribed as savouring of French, or what was held to be the same thing, revolutionary tendencies. He could not, at least at the outset of his administration, calculate with any amount of certainty or safety on the degree of reaction which the restoration of a perfectly Free Trade in corn might produce. The restored government issued its decrees prohibiting the local magistrates from interfering in the transport or sale of corn, or attempting to regulate the market in any other way except by keeping watch that the corn and flour exposed for sale were of a healthy quality, and that the weights and measures were correct. But the local magistrates in many cases refused to obey, and did everything in their power to render inoperative the grand ducal edict. The Minister of Police, Puccini, was under the necessity of addressing to the local magistrates a circular, calling upon them to desist. They continued in their opposition. Then Puccini, by Fossombroni's orders, addressed to them another and much more stringent circular, to the effect that the grand duke was quite resolved to deal most energetically and most severely with the offenders.

From that date until the rule of the dynasty of Hapsburgh-Lorraine came to a close Tuscany had no more Protectionist reactions. But if there was no more Protectionist reaction, there was something which, in the course of forty-five years, produced exactly the same result—there was Free Trade inaction ; and it is quite as possible to fall behind, or at least to lose your relative position towards the rest of the world by merely standing still when the rest of the world is marching onwards, as by deliberately turning back when the rest of the world is standing still. The restored Tuscan government, acting chiefly under Fossombroni's advice, had recalled into vigour the customs tariff of 1791. That tariff had been altered, as was already remarked, in many points in a Protective sense, and therefore contrasted unfavourably with the more liberal tariff

given by Peter Leopold ten years before. But it was
still, in its great outlines, the most liberal tariff in the
world.   Though prohibiting, as to some articles, the
export of raw materials ; though increasing the duty
on certain foreign articles of which the introduction
might be presumed hurtful to the native produce ;
it adopted and carried out as its general rule the
principle of levying a duty of 15 per cent. on the
declared value of all foreign articles imported into the
country.   Such a rate of duty was in 1791 singularly,
in 1781 portentously, liberal.   But when, in the long
period of European peace following on the French
revolutionary and Napoleonic wars, manufactures received in all countries a great development ; when, by
so many new improvements in the mechanical and
chemical processes of manufacturing industry, all goods
could be sold at infinitely lower prices ; when the relation of the profits to the capital invested by the manu-
facturer in his undertakings became completely altered ;
the Tuscan tariff, with its 15 per cent. duty, represented
less and less every day the great advance in Free-Trade
principles which it had reflected at its origin.   The new
current of manufacturing and commercial progress had
the effect of converting the Tuscan, relatively so enlightened a Free Trader at the close of the eighteenth, absolutely and virtually, at least in not a few matters, into
a Protectionist in the middle of the nineteenth century.
When all prices were very high, 15 per cent. neither
involved a marked Protective result, nor could it hold
out any very tempting premium to the smuggler.   The
general lowering in the prices of manufactured goods,
and the tenfold increased facilities which an increase
more than tenfold in the means of communication and
transport furnished to the smuggler, produced their
natural effects.   The change operated, of course, most
severely on the cheap articles most in demand.   A duty
of fifteen pounds sterling on a consignment of velvet or
lace possessing the declared value of a hundred pounds

sterling is a very different thing from a duty of fifteen shillings on a piece of printed calico possessing the declared value of a hundred shillings. In the one case it may scarcely affect the sale, in the other case it may act with a very strong Protective tendency. The Commission of the Academy of the Georgofili, in a remarkable Report —to which I shall presently refer at length—addressed by it in 1856 to the Brussels International Congress for the Revision of Customs Duties, gave great prominence to these considerations. There is a special reason for bearing them in mind at the present moment. At the meeting of the Society of French Economists, held in Paris, in the August of the year 1875, M. Clapier, in reference to proposed changes in the Italian customs tariffs, declared that the duties would in no case exceed ten per cent., which by all economists was admitted to be a fair rate. Now the difference between the Tuscan tariff of 1791 and its various modifications—for it underwent no general revision between 1814 and 1856—consisted chiefly in the fact that the scale of duties had been reduced in many cases from fifteen to twelve, eleven, and ten per cent., so that it varied from ten to fifteen—in a great number of cases being at the former figure. If, in 1856, a Tuscan tariff thus constituted was believed by the most competent authorities on the subject to have assumed, through the mere lapse of time and general change of commercial relations, a too Protectionist character, the same remark must apply *à fortiori* to any proposal for fixing, twenty years later, a kindred standard.

There was, I have observed, no further reaction against the principle or the practice of Free Trade in Tuscany. As regards the practice, one very gross exception had always existed in the duties on foreign imports—the exception was that of iron—and notice will shortly be taken of the same. But in the year 1824 (just ten years after the restoration), the immense supplies of corn from the Black Sea ports

had lowered that commodity to the price of only ten
Tuscan lire the sack, after it had fetched a price, six
and seven years before, in 1817-18, of between sixty and
seventy Tuscan lire the sack.   Many of the Tuscan
landowners became alarmed, and the question was then
mooted whether there ought not to be a sliding scale
by which the duty on foreign corn should rise with the
fall of the market price.   A keen controversy took place
on the subject amongst the members of the Academy of
the Georgofili, the cause of absolute and unfettered
Free Trade in corn being victoriously sustained by one
of Italy's greatest patriots, as well as one of her most
illustrious writers and statesmen, the Marquis Gino
Capponi.   The victory in argument, and the constantly
growing and deepening conviction in the national mind
that Tuscany had owed her economic regeneration to
Free Trade in corn, had the effect that this was the last
attempt made, even in the peaceful fields of speculation,
to overthrow the Leopoldine system.

  The economic history of Tuscany from the restoration of the House of Hapsburgh-Lorraine, in 1814, until
the fall of that House in 1859, and the union of the
State with Sardinia in the following year, requires at
least a glance at the contemporary political situation.
From 1814 until the death of Fossombroni, in 1844,
that situation was one of unruffled tranquillity, and as
compared with the other Italian, and, indeed, with many
great European States, one of truly enviable happiness.
A close observer might, indeed, have detected and
deplored the fact that the tone of the public administration was not very high, and that more attention was
bestowed on the material than on the moral wants of
the people.   Still, this amount of material comfort was,
in a great degree, the cause that the revolutions of
Piedmont and Naples found no echo amongst the
Tuscan population ; and it was almost wholly the cause
that the periodical risings in the Papal States with the
recurrence of each bad harvest only excited in Tuscany

a mingled sentiment of wonder and compassion. Even the great French revolutionary wave of 1830 broke harmless on the Tuscan State. Fossombroni's death, in 1844, seemed to be the signal for petty attempts at reaction, which became more ludicrous than hateful when the country was swept into the strong current of national feeling after the accession of Pius IX. I take occasion here to repeat the statement which I previously made—that in the negotiations for the proposed Customs League between Sardinia, Tuscany, and the Papal States, the personal leanings of Pius IX were in favour of a Free-Trade policy, and that he particularly insisted on the participation of Signor Scialoia in the negotiations, from the conviction that liberal views would be by that distinguished economist ably and vigorously represented. But mere economic interests disappeared in the troubled years 1848-9, before the more imperious influences of war, of revolution, and reaction ; and when, in 1849, Tuscany witnessed the return to Florence of the Grand Duke Leopold II., in the rear of an Austrian corps of occupation, that spectacle was but too soon followed by another—the view of Austrian diplomatists demanding from the State of Peter Leopold and Bandini the absolute and unqualified surrender of its most cherished economic traditions, in order to forward the ends of Austrian Protectionists, through the mechanism of an Austrian Customs League.

During the whole of this period, from 1814 until Tuscany ceased to exist as a separate State, in 1860, no intellectual, social, and moral force in the country contributed more constantly and more effectually to propound and diffuse sound economic doctrines than that truly illustrious body the Academy of the Georgofili. This association, so famous in the economic annals of Italy, owed its origin to the philanthropic and patriotic spirit of a Tuscan monk, Don Ubaldo Montelatici, and its first meeting, attended only by a small knot of friends, was held in Florence, on the 4th of June, 1753.

It was a happy omen for the part which a sovereign of
the House of Bonaparte was destined to play a hundred
and seven years later in the annals of Free Trade, that
in this first little group of agriculturists and economists
an Abbé Bonaparte is to be found. Don Ubaldo Montelatici's little society possessed at first more an agricultural than an economic character; but even in the first
moderate form it encountered violent opposition, based on
two maxims—first, that agriculture was not a science at
all, nor capable of scientific treatment; and, second,
that everything about it really worth knowing had long
ago been discovered. But the far-seeing monk already
beheld with his mind's eye the Liebigs of a future age,
and he was fortunate in bringing over Count Richecourt,
then at the head of the regency, to his enlightened and,
for his day, very original and startling principles. The
new Academy soon received, with the sanction of the
sovereign, an extension of its powers, and from the
commencement of Peter Leopold's reign until our own
day it discharged—the language is scarcely too strong—
many of the functions of a national representation.
For, if one excepts the questions more directly and
immediately affecting the form of government, it would
be difficult to find a subject of economic, legal, or
financial importance which has not at some time or
other been treated in the memoirs and discussions of
the body. All that vast range of inquiry which it is
the custom now to designate as social science; all the
topics connected with population, education, criminal
statistics, legal procedure, land tenure, monetary crisis,
&c., have successively engaged the attention of the
members. Tuscany has to thank them for the fact of
having had a low and uniform postage-rate long
before the genius of Rowland Hill conferred that
blessing on our own country; and that is only one
amongst many illustrations of their beneficial action.
Naturally and necessarily the peculiar conditions of
their own economic system and land tenure have ever

held the foremost rank in their inquiries. In referring to land tenure I can do nothing more than mention the long series of important inquiries respecting the *métayer* system with which the volumes of the transactions are filled. The bearings of that system on Free Trade, in the largest sense of the term—on the right and power of the landed proprietor to regulate or alter the pacts, express or tacit, legislative or customary— with the peasant cultivator of the soil, open up, in connection with land tenure, a series of questions quite as closely connected with the principles of Free Trade as the question of entail itself. Amongst the eminent Tuscans who, in the discussions of the Georgofili, have taken part for or against the *métayer* system, I shall only refer at present to the Marquis Gino Capponi as one of the leaders in the former, and the late Vincenzo Salvagnoli in the latter camp; and the mere mention of such names will, to all who are at all familiar with the annals of economic controversy in Tuscany, suffice to indicate the range of historical erudition and scientific research which their combats have exhibited.

It was just after the long period of economic prosperity enjoyed by Tuscany since the restoration of 1814 had reached its height—namely, at the close of the thirty-three years, which included ten years of the rule of the restored Grand Duke Ferdinand, and the first twenty-three years of that under his son Leopold II., that the Academy of the Georgofili celebrated one of its most memorable festivals. It was a festival of which the record possesses especial interest for the members of the Cobden Club, for it was held in honour of the great economist and statesman from whom the club derives its name, and whose task of international peace and goodwill it seeks to carry out. In the spring of 1847 Mr. Cobden, after having spent some time in Spain, visited Italy, and after being the object of numerous public demonstrations in Genoa, and Naples, and of others, not, indeed, so public, but equally cordial and

welcome at Rome, he arrived at Florence. The Academy
of the Georgofili, which only a few months before had
nominated Sir Robert Peel one of its honorary members,
held, on the 2nd of May, a public meeting in honour of
Mr. Cobden, at which he also was chosen an honorary
member of the body. On this occasion the president of
the academy, the Marquis Cosimo Ridolfi, expressed,
in the name of the members, their common satisfaction
that the economic faith, in honour of which a humble
and modest altar had so many years before been erected
in Tuscany, should now, through Mr. Cobden's apostle-
ship, have become the accepted creed of the British
people, and · be destined, through the influence of
England, to become, sooner or later, the creed of the
whole world. In referring to the actual conditions of
Tuscany at the time, the Marquis Ridolfi spoke of the
efforts of the Grand Duke Leopold II. to promote the
education of the people—efforts, he added, necessary
and laudable in any State, but especially so in one where
full and free liberty of trade in the people's food was the
first principle of the national legislation. Tuscany, the
president said, had, just like the rest of Europe, passed
through a period of great scarcity ; it had experienced—
here the Marquis Ridolfi referred to the extraordinary
fall in the price of grain which took place in 1824—the
effects of a quite exceptional cheapness, but, thanks to
the gradual growth of public opinion on economic
matters, neither the complaints of the masses in the
dearest, nor the too susceptible self-interest of some
landowners in the cheapest, times, had caused the
government and the country to swerve from their long-
established course. For these reasons he held that every
enlightened Free Trader should be a zealous promoter
of popular education—the interests of the two causes
were inseparably linked.

Mr. Cobden, in replying to this address, refused,
with his characteristic modesty, to accept for himself
the tribute of admiration offered by the president and

the members. The abolition of the Corn Laws in England, he said, had been due to three causes—first, to the fact that they had truth and justice on their side; second—and this he afterwards declared to be really the chief cause—to the accident of the Irish potato famine; and, third, to the noble sacrifice of personal and party feeling evinced by Sir Robert Peel in the complete abandonment of his former Protectionist theories. He fully echoed the belief expressed by the Marquis Ridolfi that the complete entrance of England on the path of Free Trade must involve, sooner or later, the adoption of a kindred policy by the rest of the world. The commercial interests of England, he said, were at once so vast and so varied—they affected all parts of the habitable globe—that other States must, willingly or unwillingly, find themselves drawn within the vortex of her commercial policy. He had of late had but too frequent occasion to realise in different European countries the truth of what the Marquis Ridolfi had said respecting the necessary alliance between political economy and popular education. These late sore times of famine had given rise to popular tumults in many parts of the Continent. In France alone these tumults had led to several cases of capital punishment; and all this he believed might have been averted had the people generally been more instructed in their true economic interests. Political economy of some kind, Mr. Cobden said, the people will be sure to learn; if you do not give them the teaching that is sound and good, they will themselves seek that which is worthless and pernicious. They will imbibe the teachings of Owen and Fourier, and the like absurdities. Mr. Cobden then proceeded to say that in Tuscany he had found the true principles of Free Trade so assimilated by the national mind that they had become one with the people's thought and feeling; political economy had here a heart equally with a head, and its truths exhibited no mere scientific skeleton, a full-grown, living body, all flesh and blood; and he

concluded this remarkable address with that declaration
of the preference which he always gave to the moral
over the material aspects of economic science, the
declaration which in a previous part of this sketch I
have already quoted, and which is eminently characteristic of the moral and religious tone of the speaker's
mind.

The same evening a dinner was given to Mr. Cobden
in the palace of the Marquis Ridolfi, and there the
intellectual banquet of the morning was prolonged, in
addition to the more material and substantial viands of
the feast. I doubt not that there are other readers
who will share the feeling of sadness that comes over
my own mind when, in perusing the eloquent speeches
opening the series of toasts—those in honour of the
Grand Duke Leopold II. and his son, the hereditary
Prince Ferdinand—they contrast all the hopes and
promise of that time, all the affectionate memories then
clustering around the grandson and great-grandson of
Peter Leopold, with the later fortunes of these two
princes. Had the last princes of the House of Hapsburgh-Lorraine kept steadily in mind the lessons of a
Florentine politician, far inferior to Tuscany's economic
sages Bandini and Neri in moral worth, but second to
no other statesman in a keen appreciation of the weakness
and strength of governments—had they learnt from
Machiavelli that in the conduct of a government weakness is wickedness, they might not the less, perhaps,
have been compelled, in compliance with great national
exigencies, to lay down crown and sceptre, but their
surrender of royalty would at least have been effected
under very different conditions, and have been encircled
with the same gratitude and veneration which their
names called forth at that Cobden banquet of the 2nd
of May, 1847.

The banquet in the Ridolfi palace was one at which
the company consisted entirely of men of science or
statesmen. The citizens of Florence as a body resolved

to *fête* Mr. Cobden separately ; and nothing could be more splendid than the entertainment given to him in the Borghese palace. At this second dinner, on his health being drunk by the chairman, the then Mayor of Florence, Ubaldino Peruzzi, uncle of the present mayor, who bears the same name, Mr. Cobden gave expression to the feelings with which he visited Florence by saying that to him the Tuscan soil was the sacred soil of economic freedom, and that he trod it with the feelings with which the devout Catholic approaches Rome, with which the true Moslem enters Mecca, with which the sincere Christian first beholds Jerusalem ; and with this remarkable utterance may fitly be concluded the notice of Mr. Cobden's sojourn in Florence.

That visit of Mr. Cobden to Italy was, however, productive of more important results in other parts of the peninsula. In Sardinia we shall find that the personal relations contracted with the Marquis Massimo d'Azeglio at Genoa, and Count Cavour at Turin, had no slight share in strengthening the resolution of these two distinguished statesmen to further the cause of Free Trade in their own country. How vigorously and successfully Count Cavour did so, both as Minister of Agriculture and Commerce in Massimo d'Azeglio's cabinet, and in his own character of premier after D'Azeglio's resignation, will require detailed notice. But Mr. Cobden's personal influence at Naples and at Venice was at the time more immediate and direct. At Naples his personal intercourse with Antonio Scialoia, Carlo Poerio, Pasquale Stanislas Mancini, and Carlo de Cesare, stimulated the efforts of those friends of commercial liberty ; and the last-named of these four eminent Neapolitans did full justice to the extent of Mr. Cobden's services in the able work on the great conflict between Free Trade and Protectionism published by him ten years after Mr. Cobden's visit. At Venice the most illustrious of Venetian patriots, Daniel Manin, hailed, in Mr. Cobden's visit, not only the opportunity of making a great social and civic protest

against the Protectionist tendencies of Austria, but of
constantly holding up to his fellow-citizens the example
of Mr. Cobden's recent successes in England as a proof of
the important results to be obtained from orderly and
pacific agitation in a just cause. Not that Manin for
a single moment deluded himself into the belief that
Austria could ever be driven out of the Quadrilateral
save by force of arms. But it was a very important
object for him to enlist, as early as possible, in the
moral, social, and pacific movement against Austria, as
many members as possible of those cautious and conservative classes who, though quite averse to become
the sharers in active revolutionary movements, were not
disinclined to enrol themselves as economic reformers
beneath a flag on which were inscribed the words
" Free Trade and Richard Cobden."   Count Palfi, the
Austrian Governor of Venice, quite understood this state
of matters, and had his shrewd suspicions that free
exports and imports might be, after all, only a convenient synonym for free Italians.   He could hardly be
said to sanction—he sulkily winked at the dinner given
to Mr. Cobden at the Giudecca by eighty of the leading
citizens of Venice.   These descendants and representatives of the merchant-princes of a State which had ever
been—and that sternly, almost savagely—Protectionist,
received the victor over English Protectionism, each of
the eighty hosts wearing an ear of wheat at his button-
hole.   After the speeches—as liberal in tone as the
state of Venice would permit—the eighty hosts, with
their guests, swept, in a long train of gondolas, along
the Grand Canal, to the sound of festive music.   The
English Free Trader who now visits Venice may read
there the name of Richard Cobden, written by his own
hand on one of the slabs in the Doge's palace.   He
will find it in the *loggia* or *portico* occupied during the
republic by the government officers whose special business it was to regulate the supplies of food for the State
of Venice.   There, in the very centre and citadel of old

Venetian Protectionism, it speaks with an eloquence all its own.*

In the Papal States the new pontiff, Pius IX., as already stated, had exhibited Free-Trade tendencies. But even under the reign of his predecessor, Gregory XVI., the second city of the Papal States, Bologna, had been the scene of an eloquent testimony to Mr. Cobden's triumphs. The present Italian premier, Signor Minghetti, had in the spring of 1846 read in the Agricultural Society of Bologna an interesting and eloquent memoir on the great revolution effected in the English Corn Laws. In Rome itself the commercial prospects of Italy formed, during Mr. Cobden's stay in that city, the subject of much animated discussion with the Marquis Massimo d'Azeglio. That distinguished Piedmontese statesman has left in one of his writings the record of his conversation with Mr. Cobden on the Pincio, and has told us how, when giving utterance to his regret that his native country could not exhibit the marvellous development of manufactures by steam-power seen everywhere in England, he was met by Mr. Cobden's emphatic answer, " There is your true steam-power "—and he pointed up to the glorious Italian sun, flooding Rome and the Campagna with its light—" There is your true steam-power ; what more to develop the resources of your country can you ever want ? "

It was just ten years after Mr. Cobden's visit to Italy —it was in the year 1857—that the Academy of the Georgofili published the memoir on Tuscan commercial policy addressed by it the previous year to the International Congress sitting at Brussels for the revision of customs tariffs. In complying with the request addressed

* These and other interesting details respecting Mr. Cobden's visit to Venice may be found in Professor Albert Errera's two recently-published works—his " Report on the Arts and Manufactures of Venice in Connection with the Vienna International Exhibition," and his " Daniel Manin and Venice." The first of these two works narrates the very practical form which Manin's relations with Cobden at once took—his campaign in favour of Free Trade in iron.

to it in the two Brussels circulars of 25th April and 10th July, 1856, the Academy had appointed a special commission, consisting of four members, Councillor Poggi, now Vice-President of the Court of Taxation of Florence ; Signor Marco Tabarrini, at that time Secretary of the Tuscan Council of State, and now Senator of the Kingdom of Italy ; Signor Raffaele Busacca, two years later Minister of Finance of the Tuscan Provisional Government, and now member of the Italian Chamber of Deputies ; and the late Professor Francesco Bonaini, the chief director of the Tuscan archives. Councillor Poggi had already distinguished himself in economic science as the author of a most valuable work—the general history of the laws regulating agriculture from the Roman times to our own day. Signor Tabarrini, by his very official position, had great practical knowledge of the past and present commercial legislation of his country ; Signor Busacca, as an economist, was equally marked for learning and acuteness ; and the late Professor Bonaini, if second to any contemporary Tuscan, was second only to the Marquis Gino Capponi, in the knowledge of the successive phases of Tuscan history, as reflected in the Republican, Medicean, or Hapsburgh-Lorraine annals. The joint-labours of these four academicians were embodied in a Report from the pen of Signor Busacca, at that time the acting-secretary of the Georgofili. This Report, transmitted to the Brussels Congress, possesses for the student of Tuscan commercial policy a quite exceptional value. It is an official document, emanating from a body which, at the date of its publication, had been engaged for a period of a hundred and four years in upholding the principles of Free Trade. It is the production of members of that body eminently qualified, even in their individual character, to speak with authority on this subject. It was drawn up by these persons for the purpose of being submitted to the economists and financiers of other countries—to the class best fitted to examine and estimate its conclusions.

And it was framed little more than two years before the House of Hapsburgh-Lorraine ceased to rule in Tuscany—little more than three years before Tuscany was united with Sardinia; and it may therefore be fairly considered as a kind of general summing up of all that Free Trade had done for the country, and of all that had been left undone, not by Free Trade itself, but by the defects, the shortcomings, or the difficulties, in its application.

At the risk of appearing presumptuous for hazarding such an assertion, I venture, however, on the statement that in one respect the present historical sketch, scanty and meagre as I feel its details to be, may supply a gap in the Georgofili Report. The Brussels Congress, in addressing its request to the Georgofili, observed that what it most wanted was a "statistique bonne et sérieuse ou des propositions découlant des faits, et pouvant conduire à des résultats pratiques." The Academy Report commences by at once declaring that its authors have no statistics to produce; no official statistics, they said, were at their command. Now, though it was quite true that the board of statistics established a short time before in Tuscany had been confining its labours to reports on lunatic asylums, mineral springs, foundling-hospitals, &c., and had thrown no light on the past or actual commercial changes of the country, the government, before the printing of the Report, had actually published the returns of the exports and imports of the five previous years; and the commission might at any rate have compared them with the returns of the exports given twenty years before, and then again with the returns furnished by Gianni to Count Carli, in 1757, just before the Free-Trade system came into operation. By the simple comparison of these three returns, we know that, whereas the Tuscan exports in 1757 amounted to, Tuscan crowns, 1,268,000, or, in Tuscan lire to 8,876,000, in 1837 the average annual exports of Tuscany for the five previous years amounted

G

to 38,000,000 Tuscan lire ; in the year before the Academy transmitted its Report to Brussels—in 1855—to 69,697,449 Tuscan lire. Now we saw that in 1757 the imports were estimated as nearly of the same amount with the exports. The imports of Tuscany for the year 1855 amounted to 90,196,498 Tuscan lire, giving for that year a total of exports and imports of 159,893,647 Tuscan lire. The trade both in exports and imports had, therefore, risen from a total of 17,752,000 Tuscan lire, in 1757, to a total of 159,893,647 Tuscan lire in 1855. These plain figures speak volumes. Premising thus much—and it will, at any rate, serve to invest with a more definite, positive, and concrete character the statements in the Georgofili Report—I now proceed to give an abstract of the same. After the declaration that the Academy had no official statistics at its command, and that it would be a hazardous matter for any private individual to substitute for the same the result of his individual researches, the Report begins by giving a short outline of the early conditions of the great prosperity of the Italian republics of the Middle Ages in general, and of Florence in particular, which it ascribes to the earlier and more general developments in the peninsula of the same causes which in all other European States contributed at a later period to foster national wealth and civil freedom. Just as in England, and Germany, and Flanders, the wealth consequent on trade, and the influence consequent on wealth, led to a preponderance of the manufacturing and burgher, over the agricultural and feudal element, the energy and power of the Tuscan, as of the other Italian republics, soon asserted and maintained their rights against the feudatories of the German Empire. But the freedom and power which were alternately the causes and effects of the national wealth were crushed beneath the rule of Charles V., and the Medicean domination led to that state of wretchedness which has been described at the commencement of the present essay. The Report passes still more rapidly over the periods of the Leopoldine legislation, the French occupation, and the restored Hapsburgh-Lorraine rule, under Ferdinand and Leopold II., that it may enter on the precise task which the Academy wished to perform—to give, namely, to the Brussels Customs Congress as faithful a picture as it could furnish of the condition and effects of Tuscan commercial legislation. That legislation, it stated, was animated throughout by the principle of Free Trade. There were, indeed, some important exceptions in practice to that principle, but these exceptions were condemned by the great body of Tuscan economists and financiers; and their disappearance from Tuscan commercial law was greatly to be desired. The best way, the Report said, of setting forth the extent of the commercial liberty realised in the grand duchy would be to give a complete enumeration of all restrictions on the same ; for when these were excepted, the commercial freedom of the country in every other respect was complete. These restrictions the Report then proceeded to consider under four heads :—First, Restrictions on the trade in and transfer of land ; second, Restrictions on the personal liberties of the citizens to choose and prosecute any kind of trade or manufacture ; third, Restrictions on the home trade, on the general circulation of merchandise in the interior of the country ; and, fourth, Restrictions on foreign trade.

Examining the first of these heads—the trade and transfer of land—the Report states that the only restrictions in the same are the revived form of entail, slight and insignificant as that revived form was in comparison with the system swept away, in the powers granted to attach to commanderships of the Order of St. Stephen an inalienable landed property having the value of ten thousand Tuscan crowns. The only other restriction on the transfer of property consisted in somewhat too complicated legal forms in the Tuscan law of mortgages ; though, as to mortgages in general, the Report expresses its strong doubts as to the expediency, in the real interests of commerce, of having mortgages on land at all.

Proceeding to examine the restrictions on individual liberty in the choice of any occupation, or of any commercial pursuit, the Report states that all occupations and trades are free, with the following exceptions, of which some, it will be seen, are far from unimportant :— First, No joint-stock company can be formed without the government sanction. Second, No private individual allowed to grow, manufacture, or sell tobacco on his own account, the tobacco-trade being a government monopoly. Third, No private individual allowed to manufacture or trade in salt, for the same reason. Fourth, No private individual allowed to open or work iron-mines in Elba. (This prohibition was designed to protect the State iron-mines of Elba.) Fifth, No private individual (this restriction was, of course, founded on sanitary reasons) allowed to cultivate rice without the permission of the government. Sixth, Prohibition to exercise the various branches of the legal and medical professions without the required examinations and degrees. Seventh, Certain restrictions (these, by the way it may be observed, were of very recent date, and had only been made since the Austrian occupation and political reaction of 1849) on education—at least when the teaching referred to philosophical and religious subjects. Such, then, was the entire amount of the restrictions in personal freedom in commercial matters, just at the period when Tuscany, as a separate State, with its Leopoldine legislation, was about to be merged in the common Italian country.

The Georgofili Report, whilst condemning the restrictions regarding tobacco, salt, and the Elba iron, thought that on one point, the absence of one restriction accepted in almost all other States might furnish occasion for just criticism. Though literary and artistic copyright was admitted in Tuscany, its legislation did not recognise to any extent whatever a special right of property in scientific or mechanical inventions ; no patents were acknowledged; the native Tuscan could not obtain one; the foreigner could not make good his right of patent in a Tuscan court of law.

In passing on to treat of the third division—the *restrictions on internal trade*—the Report first proceeds to give just prominence to the fact that, with exceptions about to be mentioned, no obstacles existed to free commercial circulation, especially in the matter of agricultural produce. Grain and flour of all kinds might seek and find their natural level in every Tuscan market. No restrictions hampered the baker in the making or the sale of bread, nor did any government officer interfere with the miller's trade. I suspect that more than one Tuscan miller who now receives, not always in the best possible temper, the periodical visits of the Italian tax-collector on matters relating to the grist-tax, must look back with a sigh to the times described in the Georgofili Report. Nor would the Tuscan economists who might now chance to read the next passages in that Report be inclined to think that Italy, with its present vast network of *dazi di consumo*, or *octroi offices*, has made much progress on the state of things deplored and condemned so strongly in the Report, just because it presented an unwelcome contrast to the general freedom of Tuscan internal traffic. The Report expressed the regret that when, in proceeding to abolish the 103 internal customhouses by which Tuscany was overspread in his time, Peter Leopold suppressed 99, he still allowed four— those of Florence, Siena, Pisa, and Pistoja—to remain. To these four there had been added, just ten years before the Report was drawn out, a fifth—since Lucca had become united with the Tuscan territory. The Report condemned in the strongest terms the continuance of an abuse so completely at variance with the otherwise rational system of commercial freedom in the interior. It remarked—and the remark is equally applicable to the Italian local custom-houses of the present day—that the term *octroi* would very imperfectly represent the degree of inconsistency or the amount of mischief reflected in these separate municipal tariffs. The French *octroi* was almost wholly confined in its operation to meat, vegetables, and liquors. The Tuscan *dazi di consumo* took a much wider range, so that the merchant who had already paid a duty at the frontier had to pay a second duty at the city gates— there being thus in operation within the boundaries of the State six separate customs tariffs, instead of one. It is true that the sums levied for these local customs were very small, but they did not the less involve much trouble, much delay, and much needless loss of time.

The Georgofili Report concluded by setting forth the conditions of foreign trade as determined by the tariff of 1791. Originally a Protectionist modification of Peter Leopold's more liberal tariff of 1781, this tariff had again received numerous modifications, nearly all, with one exception, in a liberal sense, since 1814. These modifications, the Report declared, were so numerous that it had become utterly impossible to follow them in detail, and precise knowledge of all the windings of this labyrinth was confined to the cus-tom-house officers of Leghorn. But, as a general rule, through the effect of the successive reductions, the duty on all imports ranged from ten to fifteen per cent. For the reasons already stated, that rate was pronounced by the Academy to be far too high for a really liberal commercial tariff, in 1856. The entire system required revision. But the chief difficulty of the revision sprang from the mistaken financial policy which derived so large an amount of the public income from such sources as the salt monopoly, the tobacco monopoly, the Elba iron monopoly, to say nothing of the lottery. A revised and improved tariff would be miserably incomplete which did not aim at a thorough reform in these departments. Bearing in mind these reservations, the Report referred to the pernicious effects of the government monopoly in Elba

iron on the foreign trade in iron manufactures. With
the view of favouring its own iron, the duty on imported
iron manufactures had long been kept as high as eighty
per cent. This enormous duty, had, however, been
reduced in 1836 to twenty-five per cent. Only in two
respects had the general standard of the tariff been raised
above fifteen per cent. This had taken place not long
before the Georgofili Report was drawn up, in the cases
of sugar and coffee, by which the duty had been raised
as high as twenty per cent. ; but the augmentation did
not promise very favourable financial results. The
Tuscan tariff, it was further stated, did not directly
recognise discriminating duties; merchandise paid duty
without any reference to the country that produced it ;
but an indirect discriminating duty existed in the
different rates of harbour dues exacted at Leghorn,
from the ships of various nations, according to the
different terms of the treaties of commerce and navigation concluded with different countries. All these duties
were levied in two forms : in the case of manufactures
generally, on the declared value ; in the case of raw
materials and many coarse articles, merely by quantity,
by weight, measure, or capacity, without any reference
to difference in the value of the articles thus taxed.
The Report touched upon the inconveniences, along with
the advantages, of both systems ; the facility afforded
by the first to trade, the unfairness often practised
in the second, by applying a common standard of duty
to articles which in reality exhibited infinite varieties of
value. In its actual operation the Leghorn customs
system was, the Report regretted, absurdly annoying and
dilatory, through the number of separate little duties,
each one in itself very small, and even in the total
amount insignificant, but not the less leading to much
trouble and loss of time. There had even, by means of
one of these little harbour duties, been recently imposed
a small, indeed a very small, tax on the corn trade ; for
the special fee for clearing corn cargoes was the sole

restriction that Tuscany for so many years had witnessed in reference to its absolutely Free Trade in
cereals.   The Academy Report terminated by recording the fresh difficulties raised up to Tuscan trade
by the recent incorporation of Modena and Parma
in the Austrian Customs League, and by the conclusion of the treaty with the Papal States, by which
Tuscany bound itself to give a more effective co-opera-
tion for the repression of smuggling along the Papal
frontier.   Now the entire land-frontier of Tuscany is
marched by the Modenese and Papal territory. The old
Modenese customs tariff had been far from a liberal one.
But, bad as it was, it was made a thousand times worse
by the total sacrifice of the Modenese consumers to the
interests of the Austrian artificially-fostered manufactures. These increased restrictions had, of course, reacted
both on the actual commerce between Tuscany and
Modena, and the commerce of transit which had previously existed between Tuscany and Northern Italy.
But the historical bearing of that Austrian Customs
League was so great, in reference, not to Tuscany alone,
but to all Italy, that I must reserve a more detailed
notice of its character and effects for a later portion of
this paper. The treaty between the Papal States and
Tuscany, for the prevention of smuggling, furnished the
occasion of most just complaint on the part of the
Tuscan economists.   The provisions of that treaty
created countless difficulties for legal traffic, entailed
great expense on the Tuscan State, and did not check
the Roman smugglers when all was done.   It is bad
enough for a country to incur great financial loss for
the sake of its own monopolists and Protectionists, but
to be forced to incur such loss for the monopolists and
Protectionists of another country is really too hard. If,
at the date of this Report, the expense of keeping up
customs-guards amounted in Tuscany to above thirty
per cent. on the whole amount received from its customs
system, the expenses along the Roman frontier had no

slight share in bringing about this result. The Report, in conclusion, dwelt on the immense benefits to both the material and the moral condition of the country which the long operation of the Free-Trade system had been the means of effecting. Agriculture had become completely regenerated under its influence, owing to the very general division of property. There was not, indeed, the large accumulation of capital by which alone important manufacturing establishments could be set on foot, but there was great and general progress in small trades, and there was everywhere a general diffusion of comfort and of well-being in the population. Such, at least, had been the general character for many years, though the Report felt bound to confess that in the last few years there had neither been the same amount of general well-being, nor the public contentment consequent on the same. As a rule, production had of late not been keeping pace with the necessities of the population. There were some points to which the Report might and did refer in explanation of these facts. It could speak of the terrible failure, during successive years, of the vintage, and of the great loss of national wealth resulting therefrom. But it could only make a distant allusion to the consequences, political and moral, financial and economic, of the Austrian occupation. But the Brussels Congress, to which this Report was addressed, could have little difficulty in interpreting some of its concluding sentences in their true sense, that an anti-national government is but another term for an insecure government, and that an insecure government, in the relations of finance and trade, implies the constant existence of a very disturbing element.

At this point, and with an exposition of views on the Tuscan commercial system possessing such deserved authority, the present sketch of Free Trade in Tuscany may fitly come to a close. On looking back we find that the point of departure was the necessity of giving food to the inhabitants of one desolate, abandoned, fever-stricken province. That necessity soon led to other requirements—to the creation of a legal and social system in which alone the conditions of Free Trade could strike root and flourish. And these requirements were found to include a complete reform of home and foreign trade—a complete alteration in the conditions of land tenure. They were found to involve, and they gradually effected, a complete revolution in the modes of thinking of the whole Tuscan people, for they dispelled the long-cherished visions of a resuscitated manufacturing and commercial greatness, such as Florence had enjoyed in the Middle Ages; and they turned the energies of the Tuscan people into a more positive and practical channel—the reclaiming of their own waste lands, and the certain gains to be derived from their new position as the first corn traders on the shores of the Mediterranean. They inspired views more comprehensive still, embracing a far wider horizon, for they called forth, in the relations of foreign policy, a declaration of perpetual amity with other countries. We have seen that these great reforms were not unaccompanied, not unchequered by great reactions, and that popular ignorance at home and military aggression from abroad, nay, that the very vacillations in the minds of the economic reformers themselves, arrested the great work that had been begun. But in more favourable conditions it sprang up afresh; and if it did not produce all the benefits which it might fairly have generated, the result was ascribed by the men most conversant with its workings, not to anything faulty in the system itself, but to the want of constancy and consistency in carrying out its details. It was marred, we have seen, by deplorable exceptions to the rule; but the economists, who knew well from what causes the prosperity of their country had sprung, did not suggest that, for the sake of harmony, the good rule should be given up for the sake of the bad exceptions; they counselled that the bad exceptions should be removed, to leave free and unfettered the working of the good rule. That was the lesson taught by the economists of the little State of Tuscany; and just at this moment it is a lesson by which the economists of the great State of Italy would do well to profit.

VI.

THE growth in Italy of views favourable to commercial liberty, the several forms which these views assume in the writings of the great Italian economists, and the extent to which their speculations were influenced by or reacted on the writers of other countries, were made familiar to all English students of political economy about half a century ago by Dr. Macculloch's masterly introduction to his edition of " The Wealth of Nations." That historical summary was subsequently expanded by the author into his comprehensive work, " The Literature of Political Economy." Even if the limits assigned to the present essay did not render the task inexpedient, little benefit could arise from the attempt to reproduce, after a most scanty and meagre fashion, statements and conclusions which have been set forth so fully in that justly popular and widely-diffused publication. The chief purpose in referring to these writings here is to record the fact that, through their continuous influence on the public opinion of Italy, most educated Italians, at the period of Mr. Cobden's visit to Italy, were, as regards Free-Trade principles, much in advance of their governments; that if anywhere Protectionist or prohibitory ideas had taken deep root, this was the case chiefly in the Papal and Neapolitan States; and even there the Protectionist sympathies of the lower classes were, as might have been expected, most closely associated with the trade in corn. The economic science of Italy had, indeed, during the years immediately preceding Mr. Cobden's visit, been even more brilliantly represented abroad than at home; for no teacher in the academic halls of Bologna or Padua could pretend to rival the European fame of Pellegrino Rossi.

The great political events of which the peninsula was the scene in 1847–8–9 appeared at first to be eminently favourable to the cause of Free Trade. It was already a great step that in the negotiations for the formation of a Customs League between Sardinia, Tuscany, and the Papal States, the new pontiff should have expressed the desire to have these negotiations conducted in a liberal spirit, and with that view, to have the distinguished economist, Antonio Scialoia, associated in the work ; and long before the close of Pope Gregory XVI.'s reign the entire system of Roman Protection—not to say pro-hibition—had found an expositor and champion in the person of Angelo Galli, who subsequently held the office of Minister of the Papal Finances ; and it must, beyond all question, have given a rude shock to the Papal financiers of the old school, of whom he was the fitting type, to find suddenly on the Papal throne a prince with views so totally different from those which they had been so long accustomed to associate with all that was safe, conservative, and orthodox.

The example extended to Naples, where politicians formed in the same school with and sharing the opinions of Scialoia, did, if not very much, at least quite as much as the short term of their influence would permit. In Sardinia Count Cavour had already distinguished himself as a writer, by the cordial welcome which he had given to Mr. Cobden's triumphs, and by the spirit of fearless and outspoken conviction, constantly illustrated to the close of his career, by which he proclaimed that the economic progress and financial prosperity of his country were inseparably bound up with the progress of Free Trade. Of the remarkable men who took a part all over the Lombardo-Venetian provinces in the rising against Austria, the most distinguished Venetian patriot of the time, Daniel Manin, had, as was previously stated, identified himself both personally and politically with

Mr. Cobden's labours; whilst the most distinguished Milanese patriot amongst all the men suddenly cast up by the force of events to the direction of public affairs, Carlo Cattaneo, was remarkable for the extreme breadth of his views on all economic questions, and for his devo-- tion to principles which he regarded as amongst the most precious heirlooms of Italian science. So far, therefore, as might be inferred from the convictions and tendencies of the men everywhere associated with the new order of things, the revolutionary movement con- sequent on the accession of Pope Pius IX. promised to be favourable to the rapid extension in the Italian peninsula of commercial liberty.

But 1849 told a very different tale. The summer of that year witnessed the occupation of Rome by the French, of the Romagna, Tuscany, Modena, and Parma by the Austrians. The Austrian occupation in these latter States had scarcely commenced before the political supremacy which it involved was employed to force upon Italy a Protectionist policy, not even pretending to pos- sess any relation with Italian commercial or financial interests, but based openly and avowedly on the settled purpose of subordinating Italian trade to the prospects of those Austrian manufacturers which the cabinet of Prince Schwarzenberg was then endeavouring artificially to foster.

In the sketch given of Free Trade in Tuscany, it has been seen how, from the first and single aim of restoring life and vigour to a desolate province, there gradually sprung up, naturally, necessarily, inevitably, a series of reforms, culminating in the declared purpose, unhappily not carried out by the reforming prince, to give political freedom to his subjects as the harmonious completion of his other efforts at regeneration. From 1849 and during the ten following years, the student of Italian history has occasion to observe, on a much larger and grander scale, alike the contrast and the confirmation of Peter Leopold's enlightened system. In the policy observed by Austria towards the Italian States he will perceive how the wish to crush political and national aspirations dictated, as the most natural means of success, a crusade against the freedom of national commerce. In the policy pursued by Sardinia, with the object of combating and counteracting those Austrian plans, he will perceive that the resources of Free Trade and the new vitality which they impart unto a people were consciously and courageously invoked by patriotic statesmen who had unswerving faith in their efforts, who, looking to the frightful financial embarrassments of their country, believed that by Free Trade they would be able to retrieve the losses they had so lately suffered, and to gain strength for the fresh contests on which they were resolved to enter.

The scheme of Austria for incorporating the Italian States with her own in an Austrian Customs League formed the first, and, after sundry unsuccessful efforts to give to the scheme a far wider extension, the last stage in the Austrian policy of agglomeration which rapidly was developed after the military events of 1849. That no time might be lost, the cabinet of Vienna, in the May of that year, opened negotiations with the little States of Modena and Parma for the purpose of uniting them to the Austrian custom system. At no distant period there followed the vigorous effort of Austria to become part, not as a German power alone, but with all her different States, of the German Confederation. Contemporaneously, or, at least, not long afterwards, commenced the attempts to unite the Papal States, Naples, Tuscany, Modena, and Parma in a political and commercial confederation under the protection of Austria, and, as regarded the commercial bearings, in complete subordination to Austrian interests.

The wide-reaching plans for swamping the German States by these Austrian additions met with such decided opposition from the President of the French Republic, Prince Louis Napoleon, and the French diplomatists at the courts of Vienna, Berlin, and Dresden gave it so clearly to be understood that further perseverance of the plan would involve the breaking out of a European war, that Austria suddenly stopped short in this the most adventurous of her diplomatic campaigns. The more restricted plan of uniting all the Italian States, with the exception of Sardinia, in a common political and commercial confederation, equally collapsed, through the resistance of the King of Naples, who on this occasion, in the arts of diplomatic fence and counterfence, fairly foiled Austria at her own weapons. The Bourbon of Naples, though firmly resolved to be Absolutist in his political and Protectionist in his commercial policy, was just as firmly resolved to practice Absolutism and Protectionism only on his own account. He contrived at the very moment when the Austrian negotiations had received the final point of signature dexterously to upset them, by coming forward with a totally different set of plans in their stead. In Tuscany, where the ministers were opposed to their sovereign on the question of a change in religious policy so reactionary as the sovereign would have wished, both ministry and sovereign were in heart averse to such a renunciation of the Leopoldine Free-Trade principles as would have been effected by the entrance of the Tuscan State into an Austrian Customs League. So, at the commencement of 1852, the Austrian designs had virtually shrunk down to their original proportions of May, 1849, and the Customs League, concluded in 1852, only included the two States of Modena and Parma. In all these negotiations Austria put forth with the greatest prominence, without the least reservation, the proposition that the growth of Free Trade in Italy was identical with the progress of the Revolutionary, as it was the fashion to term the anti-Austrian, or national, movement. In this sense both Prince Schwarzenberg and his successor in the Austrian premiership, Count Buol, were constantly writing to the Duke of Modena. Cheap calicoes were the commercial form of the great

English and Sardinian conspiracy.   The Italian who preferred the interests of Italian consumers to those of Austrian producers was a declared enemy of all thrones and altars.   Strange feelings involuntarily rise up in the mind of the English reader, and memories in which politics have little part, when he comes on the letter, addressed, on the 15th of October, 1853, by Count Buol to Francis V. of Modena, where the Austrian premier informs the sovereign of Modena that the Italian railway concessions obtained by the agents of MM. Strahan, Paul, and Co. were the last phase of England's revolutionary propaganda, and that the duke's brother sovereign of Parma must be warned without loss of time as to their real character, and how seriously they endangered all sound conservative interests in northern and central States.

Such, during the period from 1849 to 1859, were the attitude and aims of Austria in the Italian peninsula in reference to all questions of commercial policy.   They require to be brought into full relief, if we would correctly appreciate the attitude and objects of Sardinia in her counter-action.   As far back as 1844 a question of customs duties on wines between Sardinia and Austria had swollen up to the proportions of a serious political conflict.   When, therefore, Mr. Cobden, three years later, at the close of his Italian tour, reached Turin, and was there *fêted* by the chief representatives of a liberal commercial policy, the demonstrations made in his honour possessed a liberal character quite as marked as those of which he had been the object only a few days before at Venice.   I have already stated that Count Cavour took a prominent part in this Turin festival, and I may now add that the whole tenor of the speech made by him at the dinner given to Mr. Cobden was a recommendation of the immense benefits to be derived from legal agitation, from the perseverance and the constancy in a just and noble cause, which Mr. Cobden had illustrated in his anti-Corn Law campaign.   These were prominently held up for the imitation of the Italian people. With reference to the personal qualities of the illustrious guest, Count Cavour addressed to him the words—and they will find an echo in the hearts of all who ever had the privilege of knowing Mr Cobden—"*De loin on vous admire, de près on vous aime!*" The influence which Count Cavour was destined to exercise on the commercial prospects of Italy was, I may further take occasion to observe, already foreshadowed by the importance which the patriots of the other Italian provinces evidently attached at this period to his writings; for we find them, years before he became a minister of the Sardinian Crown, or even a member of the Sardinian Parliament, constantly quoted with admiration and assent by the men who, in the other parts of Italy, were labouring in the cause of commercial reform. It was, therefore, only natural that when the Italian revolution had reached that further stage in which, after the success of the Austrian arms, the Sardinian Parliament was regarded as the chief bulwark of national liberty and progress, the first utterances of Count Cavour on commercial policy in the Chamber of Deputies should have been attentively weighed and be still gratefully remembered.

Economic theories so strange and startling in their nature—strange and startling, at least, to those who fondly believed in the general acceptance throughout Italy of Free-Trade principles—have recently come so suddenly to the foreground on the stage of Italian politics, that it becomes necessary to set forth, with some fulness of detail, what were the views entertained on the subjects of Free Trade and Protectionism by the great statesmen who mainly contributed to found a free, independent, and united Italy. The parliamentary speeches of Count Cavour on commercial policy are given at full length in the great collection of his parliamentary discourses, published by order of the Chamber of Deputies. That collection must be consulted by all who desire to obtain accurate knowledge respecting his parliamentary labours at the fountain-head. But an excellent summary of his speeches on commercial policy has been given by his intimate friend during the last years of his life, his confidential secretary, the accomplished diplomatist who now fills the post of Secretary-General in the Italian Ministry of Foreign Affairs, M. Louis Artom. M. Artom's work, "*L'œuvre Parlamentaire du Comte de Cavour*," possesses so deserved a reputation, and is so generally accessible, that for general convenience I prefer quoting from his pages those passages on Count Cavour's great measures of commercial reform, in which may be found reflected with most fidelity the principles by which he was guided. But before quoting these passages, it may be as well to state that the customs tariffs of Sardinia of 1830 had been of so Protectionist a character that its Protectionism might not unfairly be described as but the synonym of prohibition. Various measures of reform had been introduced between 1830 and 1850, and the successive degrees in which by these various measures a greater liberality had been imparted to the Sardinian tariff, are set forth very clearly in the reports addressed to the Sardinian Chamber of Deputies and Senate, on which the D'Azeglio Ministry (Count Cavour held the post of Minister of Agriculture and Commerce in that cabinet) based its proposals. The reports addressed to the Senate are peculiarly valuable, whether regarded from an historical or a logical point of view. Most English readers, however, will probably be of opinion that the little space reserved by the limits of this essay may be best employed in giving prominence to the declarations of Count Cavour himself.

Count Cavour, in exposing the economical principles of the ministry, and the general rules adopted for the application of those principles, stated that the government frankly declared itself Free Traders, observing that, in a normal state of affairs, the government ought not to protect, by the imposition of duties, this or that manufacture ; that it is not obliged, and that, consequently, it has not the right, to favour one or several manufactures, to the prejudice of other natural trades; that it is not fair to burden the great mass of consumers with taxes created in favour of certain branches of industry; that the custom-houses can only be established for a financial purpose—that is to say, in the interests of the public. He, moreover, added that, however advantageous to the finance custom-house duties may be, it is not fair—indeed, it is wrong—that they should weigh on all citizens for the benefit of a single class.

Count Cavour, in demonstrating how the truth of these principles had been widely explained in Italy and elsewhere, observed that if Protectionism had enjoyed and continued to enjoy the sympathy of several peoples, the reason must be found in the fact that these peoples were led to believe that Protection created the great capital employed in private manufactures. The partisans of that system generally believe that if Protectionist duties had not been established, capital would never have been formed. This, Count Cavour added, was a gross error. Protection has not the power of creating capital. It is very evident that Protection cannot allege as a defence the necessity of giving employment to capital in certain protected branches of industry, unless it can first prove that capital cannot absolutely be employed in these branches of industry—agriculture and commerce—which have no need of protection.

Count Cavour demonstrated that, so far as Piedmont was concerned, agriculture had not absorbed all the capital which might be employed to the great benefit of the country. With regard to silk, Count Cavour stated that this was precisely one of the manufactures which had been most protected in Piedmont. We had reached the point of prohibiting the exportation of raw silk. And what had the result been? The result had been that this manufacture, which in the last century had attained a remarkable superiority, has now come to a standstill—so much so that, after the Restoration of 1814, not only have we lost the priority on the market of Lyons, but we have been left far behind. After the Restoration the Sardinian government, counselled by enlightened men, attempted to stop the evil by abolishing prohibition. The question was seriously discussed under King Charles Felix, but great opposition was made, and the Chamber of Commerce of Turin, in raising the cry of Protection, addressed a memorial to the king, in which it stated that the liberty of exporting raw silk would certainly have proved a ruinous calamity. King Charles Albert succeeded in overcoming the opposition of the Protectionist party, and, in spite of great resistance made by the Council of State, the exportation of raw silk was allowed, with a moderate duty. The result was not that which the Chamber of Commerce of Turin had anticipated. New manufactories were opened, the means of manufacturing were ameliorated ; and it is now a well-known fact that the manufacturers of Turin have purchased in the London markets woven silk which had already been exported into England.

Count Cavour then proceeded to narrate how, under King Charles Felix, discriminating duties had been established on four different articles, one of which was corn, in order to protect the Genoese navigation. The duties had been fixed in a manner to insure to the national marine the importation of corn from the Black Sea and Turkey. The result was that the whole maritime commerce of Genoa took to speculate on corn, and the current was such that the results for each individual became insignificant. Then several among the Genoese thought well to escape from the clutches of Protection, and to brave competition in the free seas of America ; and very soon a considerable commerce arose between Genoa and South America. This commerce prospered far more than all others, though both were carried out by men of the same country, and, in all likelihood, of the same capacity ; but in one case there was Protection, the other was protected by liberty.

Count Cavour, in combating the reasons given by the Protectionists in defence of their principles, said, " Well, in conclusion, this is what you say : We are inferior to foreign producers ; compensate this inferiority by a prohibition which will protect us." They might be right ; they might ask time to place themselves on a level with others if foreign manufacture remained stationary—if in England, in Belgium, in France, production made no progress. But the worst is that, while our producers, under the action of Protection, move slowly along, those of foreign countries advance with the vigour of youth, of energy, and manhood ; these are stimulated by competition, the others are weakened by privilege and Protection. The same lamentations were made in France when the reforms of the customs duties were first spoken of. Protection triumphed again, but manufactures made no progress. Count Cavour, in answering Count Revel, traced the history of the economic reforms of England, and declared his astonishment at hearing the Protectionists of Piedmont invoke the example of the United States of America.

" What does that prove ? " said Count Cavour. " It proves that those people, though republicans, knew not how to give up personal to public interest, and that republican forms of government are not sufficient to tear selfishness from the human heart.

" No nation in the world offers an example favourable to Protection. On the contrary, all the enlightened men of Europe are all on the side of Free Trade, and the truth of that doctrine has penetrated as far as the Vienna Cabinet."

Count Cavour then proceeded to state how the government intended applying the principles of Free Trade. Of course, the country would not march direct from Protection to Free Trade. Great interests are now at stake, and a sudden change might bring about a disturbance, and even serious embarrassments. It is, therefore, the duty of the government to be cautious in the application of the system, and to have constantly in mind the effects of a long system of Protection. Count Cavour, in defending the government from the attack made by Count Revel against the treaties of commerce, said that the fact of having concluded similar alliances with certain nations, was one of the great merits in their line of conduct. If the ministry had no complete faith in Free Trade ; if, like Count Revel, it considered it a novelty on which experiments might be made, the system of making treaties of commerce might be dangerous. "But," added Count Cavour, "if the Chamber shares our opinion, if it has faith in Free Trade, it will be grateful to the ministry for having torn from the Protectionist party all means of throwing us back from the path of liberty." Count Cavour explained at length the importance of the treaties concluded with several nations, more particularly recommending the one concluded with England.

The same question was discussed in the sitting of April 15th. Count Cavour, while defending the principles of Free Trade, said, " With the present system the consumers pay three different taxes ; one goes into the hands of the government, the second into those of smugglers, the third in the strong boxes of privileged producers. A reform, and a radical one, must be found at once. The national treasury may lose by it, but the country at large will certainly gain ; in short, the wealth of the treasury is in proportion to that of the country." In signalling the remarkable tendency of our age to push forward in the path of political and economical reforms, Count Cavour observed that one of the objects of society at the present day is, unquestionably, that of ameliorating the condition of the lower classes. There are two means of doing so. Some have faith in liberty, in the efficacy of Free Trade, in the spontaneous development of the intellectual and moral faculties of man ; they believe that the constant application of the principles of liberty will create a general well-being, which will more especially prove beneficial to the poorer classes. Another school professes opposite principles; it believes that the miseries of humanity cannot be redressed, that the condition of the working classes cannot be ameliorated except by a systematic restriction in the exercise of individual forces, by an illimitable extension of the central action of the social body at large, represented by a government formed by the concentration of all the individual forces. " The only means," said Count Cavour, " to combat this school which menaces to invade Europe, is that of opposing principle to principle. In economy, as in politics or religion, ideas may struggle against ideas; for a time cannons and bayonets may keep truth silent, and preserve material order, but if these truths succeed in gaining the mastery of the enlightened classes, sooner or later this triumph changes the face of the world."

Count Cavour here observed that the Protectionist phase of economic theories was, in reality, the most powerful ally of Socialism. " They have started from the same principle. If reduced to its simplest expression, Protection affirms the right and the duty of a government to intervene in the distribution and the employment of capital. If these theories were to prevail, what would we reply to the working classes if they came and told us, ' You believe it is your duty and your right to meddle with the distribution of capital, and to regulate its action ? Why, then, don't you meddle with the other element of production—salary ? Why don't you regulate salary ? Why don't you organise work ? ' In truth, it appears to me that, admitting Protection, one must necessarily admit the greater part of the socialistic ideas, if not all of them."

Such are some of the most salient passages in Count Cavour's great speeches on commercial reform. It will be seen that they coincide exactly in their comments on the necessary connection between Protectionism and Socialism with the remarkable utterances made to the same effect by Mr. Cobden in his speech, addressed to the Academy of the Georgofili, on the 2nd of May, 1847. What Count Cavour then said on the tendencies of modern society to surrender to the central power of the State all individual forms of initiative and energy, has, unhappily, lost nothing of its importance at the present moment. Indeed, we are just now, in March, 1876, witnessing the reassembling of an Italian Parliament in which the prominent question to be discussed is that of the expediency for the State to take into its own hands many of the forms of commercial activity at present reserved to private speculation and action. Commercial reforms introduced by Count Cavour may be best estimated by a glance at the following statistical tables :—

COMMERCE OF THE KINGDOM OF SARDINIA, EXCLUSIVE OF LOMBARDY, IN THE LAST YEAR, 1859. IN OTHER WORDS, OF PIEDMONT, THE LIGURIAN PROVINCE, AND THE ISLAND OF SARDINIA. VALUE, ACCORDING TO OFFICIAL DECLARATIONS, OF THE IMPORTS AND EXPORTS, IN FRANCS.

| YEAR. | GENERAL TRADE. | | SPECIAL TRADE. | |
	Imports.	Exports.	Imports.	Exports.
1850	—	—	111,870,106	93,868,956
1851	—	—	129,789,533	73,133,389
1852	332,655,000	236,619,000	166,608,684	89,426,753
1853	333,942,000	220,630,000	188,020,508	95,014,264
1854	312,429,000	214,883,000	199,912,351	109,710,449
1855	315,10,5499	228,536,321	206,961,455	131,977,943
1856	390,047,098	290,635,704	244,903,388	156,192,354
1857	400,623,551	289,777,826	236,917,368	135,604,547
1858	404,610,602	307,181,313	247,332,666	159,433,471
1859	375,648,691	228,858,405	244,603,165	130,657,789

In reference to the above tables the following explanatory remarks must be given :—

Before 1851 the goods introduced into the province of Nice, or exported from that province, were not included in the official statistics, because exempted from duties.

The general commerce comprehended the special commerce, and, in addition, the carrying trade in its two phases—namely, both on entering and leaving the kingdom.

The special trade was formed by imports for home consumption, or of raw materials to be manufactured in the country, or by the export of national produce, or of such produce as might be termed nationalised in consequence of having paid the regular customs duties on entering the kingdom, or without having paid any duty, assuming that the merchandise was of such a character as to be exempt from the same.

In estimating these commercial results, we ought to keep constantly in mind the following most important facts, that during these very years Sardinia, like the rest of Italy, suffered dreadfully by the failure of one most important branch of national wealth—the wine crops ; that the trade in Black Sea corn was utterly disturbed by the Crimean War ; and that in the political attitude assumed by Sardinia, including its participation in the Crimean War, the financial resources of the State were most sorely tasked to meet all the efforts by which Count Cavour was striving directly to prepare his country for its glorious liberation. If these circumstances remove the commercial progress of Sardinia from the ordinary conditions of national commerce—and to the above causes must be also added the forced union of Modena and Parma in the Austrian Customs League —other causes, rendering quite impossible, without such inquiries as even the highest statistical authorities have not ventured to undertake to set forth with the required exactness, the difference in commercial results between the trade of united Italy and of the several States of which previous to the union it was composed. This will be at once understood when we recollect that as the trade of Lombardy was included in the general trade of the Austrian Empire, there exist no data for marking the difference, when the connection between Lombardy and Austria ceased, between the Lombard trade under the Austrian Protectionist and again under the Italian Free-Trade system. As regards Modena and Parma, exactly the same remark holds good. We know that their trade became greatly dwarfed by the operation of the Austrian Customs League, but we cannot state the exact proportions to which it expanded under the Free system, of which it only formed a part, just because for the exact proportions between that part and the whole there are no reliable data. The same remarks apply, with equal or greater force, to the commercial statistics of the Neapolitan, Sicilian, Venetian, and Roman provinces, before and after their several annexations. Some slight idea of the difficulty of coming to any satisfactory conclusion respecting the various elements, and their increase or decrease of national wealth in Italy during this period, may be formed from a single instance. The inquiries of the late Secretary-General of the Ministry of Agriculture and Commerce, Signor Maestri, a statistician whose premature death Italy has much reason to deplore, gave the value of all the wine grown in Sicily at a certain sum. His calculations form the basis of the separate official statements made regarding Sicilian wines in the official account published of the Italian wine trade at the London Exhibition of 1862, at the Paris Exhibition of 1867, and even so late as the Vienna Exhibition of the year before last. Yet as far back as the year 1864, when the present premier, Signor Minghetti, was occupied with his plans for a re-arrangement of the taxes, the Chamber of Commerce of Palermo published a very important document, to the effect that all these calculations respecting Sicilian wines were utterly worthless, because, to the certain knowledge of the Chamber, the wine grown in the province of Palermo alone was equal to the amount ascribed to the entire island of Sicily. The only means of obtaining even an approximate estimate—one, I mean, that can really be relied on—of the effects of Free Trade on the kingdom of Italy, must be preceded by an operation which has not yet been dreamt of, by such combined and systematic inquiries of all the several Chambers of Commerce as may furnish the data for a general and comprehensive body of Italian commercial statistics.

The one great and cheering fact respecting the commercial progress of the kingdom of Italy under the system of Free Trade inaugurated by Count Cavour in the kingdom of Sardinia, and afterwards extended to the other Italian provinces, is the following :—That Italy, while compelled by the exigencies of her political position to keep up, until she obtained possession of Venice and the Papal States, an immense standing army ; though equally compelled—or, at least, supposing herself compelled—by the conditions required for the establishment of the national unity, to incur enormous expenses for the creation of a vast system of national railroads ; though voluntarily burdening herself for the wise and legitimate object of political conciliation with an amount of pensions to the retired or removed functionaries of the six reactionary governments annexed to the kingdom of Sardinia ; though compelled to toil on under these truly discouraging difficulties, has yet with each successive year been able to make greater progress, and to record an unquestioned development in every branch of commercial activity. The whole secret of this success is to be found in the resources and the energies derived from freedom ; but that success would be infinitely greater if those resources and energies obtained a more unfettered play, and if civil equally with political freedom were effectually secured. As these concluding remarks on the commercial and industrial state of Italy have no more ambitious scope than to refer generally to the subject as bearing on that history of Free Trade in Tuscany which has been more fully handled, it may be said that the actual condition of Italy presents far more numerous points of resemblance to certain phases of Tuscan history than would at first sight appear. We have seen how the starting-point of our Tuscan narrative was the necessity of giving a healthy population to a most unhealthy district, which, for want of such a population, could not be cultivated, and the further necessity of raising the character of that population by wise laws wisely administered. Kindred problems present themselves at the present moment to the statesmen of the kingdom of Italy as they did 140 years ago to the statesmen of the grand duchy of Tuscany. The question whether the Roman Campagna shall be freed from its desolating malaria and made susceptible of all the agricultural improvements of which it is capable ; the question whether similar results shall be obtained in the Island of Sardinia ; the question whether the Tavoliere della Puglia shall be rendered a source of infinite wealth to Southern Italy ; and the question whether Sicily, which under its Greek and Roman masters not only nourished its own population of twelve millions, but was able to furnish corn to the whole of Italy, shall remain in its present dwarfed proportions, supplying often with difficulty its two millions of inhabitants with food. These questions are for Italy of a magnitude not inferior to that raised by Bandini and Pompeo Neri respecting the means of transforming the fever-stricken swamps and marshes of the Sienese Maremma into a flourishing and fertile territory ; and the further question, by what means the state of terrorism in the Neapolitan and Sicilian provinces, under which the Camorra and the Mafia now levy their black mail on all classes of society, may be abolished, is just as important as the question how the special privileges of the Sienese and Florentine baronial fiefs enabled every retainer of the feudal lord to thwart the course of law, and how the monstrous perogatives granted to religious orders interfered with every phase of industrial and commercial life. In the letter which I had the honour of addressing to the Cobden Club a few months ago, I gave a brief outline of the manner in which a party really Protectionist in tendency, as it seems to me, though rejecting the name, had recently sprung up in Italy, of the causes of its partial success, and of the importance of taking it into account in any careful estimate of the commercial conditions of the Italian State. Since the publication of that letter, if such tendencies have been emphatically disclaimed, and by none more strongly than by the critics of the letter in question, the general course of Italian politics has, however, served to furnish a more complete confirmation of its statements. The confirmation threatens indeed, at the moment of my penning these concluding sentences, to take the form of embittered party conflict. On the re-assembling of the Italian Parliament, programmes in which the right, the duty, and the expediency of the State to concentrate within its own hands many forms of industrial and commercial activity at present entrusted to private enterprise, will be confronted by the assertion that, to quote the language once held by Fossombroni, "Government should leave people as much as possible to look after their own business ; for every man knows and does his own business far better than any government can know or do it for him."

It is no business of mine in the present sketch, or in any other way, to enter the lists as a combatant on either side in the purely political and party contests of Italian politicians ; but I may at least, in closing this paper, be permitted to give expression to the hope that the result of these contests may be in accordance with the aims and aspirations, with the lives and labours, of Sallustio Bandini and Adam Smith, of Count Cavour and Richard Cobden.

Rome, March 4, 1876.

CASSELL PETTER & GALPIN, Belle Sauvage Works, London, E.C.